THE LION IN THE LABYRINTH

AND OTHER STORIES

by

Jane Jago

Every action provokes a reaction... From a reimagining of the Minotaur Myth to the selfishness of a man who fakes his own death, these stories consider consequences - usually unforeseen

THE LION IN THE LABYRINTH

In the black basalt rock beneath the palace, there exists a labyrinth so complex that no-one has ever fathomed its secrets. It was made, they say, by those whose machinations broke the sanity of the Great Lion and petrified a hundred hundred janissaries whose duty it had been to guard the Golden Throne and its occupant.

Whatever the truth may be, the Labyrinth had imprisoned The Lion for as long as even the sphinx could remember. The maddened king was contained by wards of strong magic as well as by locks and stone walls...

It was the first day of a new year and a young girl in a rose-coloured gown, with the black silk of her hair unbound about her, was pushed unceremoniously through the door of the labyrinth. Those who closed the door behind her with a clang had no pity for youth and beauty. The Labyrinth was her fate, as it had been the fate of so many before her. A young body would satisfy the lust of the king's beast and her blood would feed the clamouring stones.

But something went wrong. No screams rent the air and the channels in the rocky floor ran only with clear water.

How could it be that a female capable of surviving the lusts of the Labyrinth had slid past the eyes of The Family? There was disquiet. This creature was not what they had bargained for at all. Too intelligent. Too independent. Too sharply unafraid. It shouldn't have mattered that she survived, even though she wasn't meant to be any more than a tasty morsel to temporarily slake the bloodlust of the Great Lion and quench the thirst of the unknowable tunnels in which he dwelt. It shouldn't have mattered.

It wasn't as if all the women died. Through the centuries one or two had survived, through guile or pure luck. She, like them, should have been given a present of money and sent away. But this was different, The Lion called her his queen, and the Labyrinth knew her name.

So it mattered. She mattered, and everything she did mattered.

She knew no fear of The Lion and he doted on her. The watchers looked on in unbelief as his beast curled about her slender form. They said he laid his head among her silken skirts and purred like a kitten.

The Dark Master, who ruled the kingdom until such time as the stone janissaries reclaimed their fleshly bodies and a new Lion arose to claim the Golden Throne, thought to refuse her entry to the Labyrinth. But when the appointed time came, and he would have stayed with his grimoires and arcane manuscripts, he found his feet taking him to the iron-bound door and his palm touching the lock stone through no volition of his own. The Labyrinth decreed that she be allowed to enter, and as long as she lived he would admit her each evening will he or nil he.

The powerful ones grew angry in their castles and lairs. How could the world turn if there was no ravening beast to feed the stones of the labyrinth? Nails and claws extended from supposedly human hands, and priceless tapestries were shredded, as rising beasts demanded mastery.

In time, though, even they banded together, agreeing there was only one possible course of action. The 'queen' must die. Before her influence on the king's majesty became unbreakable.

It should have been easy to kill a young woman whose only power lay in the infatuation of a dangerously mad king. A junior lion was sent to her rooms with a single blade and a single purpose. He gave her no time for reaction, but as he raised his knife to slash her throat he looked into her eyes. His heart failed him and he ran. It is commonly believed that his mother ate that craven heart, taken still beating from his breast.

The enraged beasts sent their strongest and most experienced assassin, a dark and emotionless dragon who had more kills to his name then there were jewels in the crown of the caged king. He accepted the commission with a thin-lipped and contemptuous smile. He never returned, though his heart was sent to his employers in a silver box decorated with runes of such power that the priesthood wouldn't even allow it to be buried.

There were, of course, more attempts, until even the most feral beast came to understand that the rose-clad queen was possessed of protection beyond their strength to resist.

And so it continued, each night at lamp lighting a slender figure clad in rosy silks was admitted to the lair of the unchained king, and every morning she was waiting when the Dark Master came to set her free.

He hated her for being everything a female should not be, and each morning his white eyes bored into her serene brown gaze. Day on day his hatred grew more corrosive, although the lady seemed not to see him or feel any fear of his wrath.

As the year drew on, the king remained quiet in his labyrinthine prison and his avowed queen kept her own council as she moved about her day.

The Dark Master, on the other hand, grew more and more angry and more and more bitter. He became as thin as a knife blade and as dangerous to encounter. Only his life mate dared cross his path and even she was wary of his claws.

One evening he returned from the loathed nightly duty of placing his hand on the stone that admitted the Rose Queen to the increasingly hungry maw of the labyrinthine living rock to receive a not entirely pleasant surprise. There were beasts at the place he called home. Uninvited beasts. His mate stilled the angry words he would have spewed with a hand across his mouth.

"Listen," she said and something in her voice made him do as she asked.

An old dragon, whose scales rustled as he moved, blew out a small rusty looking flame.

"This so-called queen cannot be allowed to live. As long as she remains in life the Lion and the Labyrinth are in her thrall. And we grow old."

The whisper of agreement was like the winter wind in the forests that ringed the black rock within whose twisted breast dwelt the Lion.

"Indeed we do. But how can we fight this creature of earth and sky? One whose very being is all we despise."

"All we despise?" a young firedrake spoke the question many thought but left unsaid.

The Dark Master's lips twisted in a bitter sneer.

"Yes. Everything we hate. Flowers, springtime, and mortality. We believe her to be the incarnation of a minor goddess of the earth, come, somehow, in response to the dying agony of the Labyrinth's victims..."

"Oh. Then we are doomed."

"Unless we can kill the creature we are. But how may one such die?"

The dragon laughed, and it was a sound to chill the air in one's lungs.

"We have searched in every library, and panned through the memories of every living priest and seeress..."

"Some even survived the process." The snake who spoke wove sinuous coils about a black marble pillar on which burned the flame of the labyrinth. "See how sickly is the flame from which we draw life. We must prevail."

The dragon cut her off with a sickly flame of his own.

"This is known. What may not be is that this very week the lady moon will be darkened for a time by the shadow of our own planet."

"Yes. Yes. It is called an eclipse." The Dark Master was impatient.

"So it is. But what men call it is of no importance. What does matter is that this so-called queen will be in the Labyrinth with the Lion when the moon stops shining. And if we can extinguish the torches in the tunnels there will be no light. Without light she is doomed."

"Doomed?"

A cowled figure whose bent and twisted hands were clawed with razor-sharp nails giggled insanely. "The prophecies tell us that only in total darkness will the Labyrinth regain its understanding of purpose and claim its own. Then we shall have our immortality once more."

The Dark Master felt his blood rise as it had not done for many centuries. "Consider it done."

The uninvited faded away leaving The Master to face his mate. He supposed he should have been angry that she had allowed so many to approach their lair, but he could feel nothing but relief.

"Soon, my pretty," he breathed.

She touched her lips with a tongue grown suddenly forked and looked at him with slumbrous eyes.

"Soon."

As the night of the dark moon approached, The Master made certain secretive preparations and by the time he admitted the lady to her fate he was as ready as he could be.

The watcher at the Labyrinth gate was a convicted murderer, known for unthinking brutality, who had chosen to have his tongue cut out and his eardrums stabbed rather than die at the talons of the watch dragon who guarded the black mountain. He watched the Dark Master with bright, vicious eyes, but when he looked at the queen in her roseate glory his gaze grew heavy with unslaked desire. The dark one smiled sourly inside his hood, and promised the watcher a slow lingering death for this presumption. It was one thing for The Family to decide that this female must die, it was quite another for a paroled felon to lust after her white limbs.

The lady walked quietly into the dimness and, presumably, into the waiting arms of her bestial lover. The Dark Master left the catacombs walking carefully and taking the utmost care not to show that which burned and bubbled in his blood.

It was beyond darkness when the watch dragon bellowed thrice and a shadow crawled across the face of the moon.

In his draughty lair high on the mountain, a hooded figure spoke a word of power, and the torches in the Labyrinth grew pale and sickly before dying one by one. As the last torch was extinguished, black shadow completely obscured the moon's silver face.

For an instant the world held its breath, before everything was shattered by a scream that spoke of agony beyond comprehension. It went on for what seemed like a very long time, and no creature that heard it would ever be completely free of its memory.

At the gate to the labyrinth, the watcher held his hands over his ears. He might once have wished to hear again, but not so his brain could be cicatrised by another's pain.

It is not easy to cut your own throat, but when the alternative is that scream...

Morning came, with a pale sky and a crisp frost. The Dark Master walked purposefully to where the Labyrinth awaited. He poked the bloodless body of the watcher with a disdainful foot before placing his hand on the lock stone.

The gates opened with a screech of protest. No rose clad figure walked out. He waited a while before setting his feet to make the traverse into the Lion's den.

It was not a journey he had made before although his feet seemed to know their direction. His cold heart beat loudly in his chest as he walked carefully forward. The room he finally came to was surprisingly spacious, with high east-facing windows, and this morning it was a brightly lit scene of carnage. The walls and floor were liberally spattered with bright scarlet, or darker stains he didn't care to think about, while something rosily pink and ruined was draped across the stone of what he assumed was the Lion's bed. As the dark one moved closer he wondered, with a frisson of real fear, where the insane beast that was The Lion might be hiding, but he could detect no sound and his need to see that the woman was really dead overcame his terror.

He put out a hand to touch what should have been flesh only to find it was no more than rose-coloured silk covering a thing of straw and hanks of human hair. He had been tricked and the sound of laughter echoed around the hellish room. It took a few seconds for his body to catch up with his mind, and make his feet turn towards the doorway and the possibility of freedom. But even as his boots slipped and scrabbled on whatever besmirched the floor he heard the sound of his own doom.

Many floors above, in the throne room, with a sound of splitting stone the king's army of janissaries regained their mortal form and each one bowed so that his forehead touched the floor. The door beyond the throne opened with a whisper that shook the palace walls, while a breeze smelling of roses blew through the corridors clearing away the last vestiges of incense and dark majick. The tall figure of The King arrived, with as little ceremony as if he had only left the room moments ago. His leonine head bore the diadem of a thousand lights and in his right hand he carried the sword of judgement. On his left walked his beloved, crowned with diamonds and clad as ever in rosy silks.

They ascended the twin thrones and His Majesty roared.

Deep underground, the iron-banded door to the Labyrinth slammed closed with an ear-splitting screech.

The Dark Master was trapped. His beast rose to the surface, but it was deadly afraid, and when they felt hot carnivorous breath on the back of their neck, neither 'human' nor 'animal' could stop the scream that tore through their body and left their mouth in an unending ululation of despair.

The voice of the Lion reverberated in the bones of his beast as the Dark Master understood what his fate was to be.

"Welcome to your new home, brother."

Then the Lion was gone from his prison, leaving only ghostly female laughter to keep his sibling company throughout eternity.

BLOOD FEUD

Two wealthy men. For the benefit of identification we shall call them Westmorland and Cumberland.

The pair met at Eton, where the bitterness of their enmity had its root. Nobody knew what had made them such malevolent foes, or if they did they weren't telling, but by the time Westmorland was thirty-five, with a wealthy wife, who he had no problem leaving in the fastness of the grim castle that was his family home, and a couple of hopeful children, it had become the driving force of Cumberland's life. Whatever Westmorland had he must take from him. Or die in the attempt.

The final straw came in the form of a woman; a woman one man wanted and another man had. She was a beautiful opera dancer, who went by the soubriquet of Belladonna, and who had been in the habit of supplementing her income by dealing with the needs of various wealthy young men - until she became Westmorland's latest mistress. He decked her out in pearls and lace and set her up in a slim house with a view of Vauxhall gardens.

Cumberland immediately determined to take her for himself - even though he was but newly wed to a young woman of impeccable lineage and superlative beauty.

He sent flowers, with a single diamond earring at the centre of the bouquet. He sent a tiny dog with a diamond bracelet around its neck. And he began to haunt the places Westmorland and his light o' love could be found.

Westmorland watched his machinations with mild amusement, and the lady treated his advances with the disdain they probably merited.

"No signore," she was heard to observe, "l'uomo non ama nessuno tranne il suo nemico."

Those fluent in Italian wondered at the perspicacity of a puta from the stews of Florence, in that she was perhaps the first to see Cumberland's obsession as an expression of rejected love. This insight having been noted, society watched the sullen simmering hatred with a bright pitiless eye.

The only person who couldn't watch with anything approaching equanimity was Cumberland's exquisite wife. That lady's pride was quite as high as her husband's and, once she realised he really was obsessed with his enemy's mistress, she took steps. Cumberland returned home from a night at the theatre, where he had not heard a word of the play, being wholly occupied in watching Belladonna with hot covetous eyes, to find his wife gone.

He twisted his handsome, sardonic face into a sarcastic half smile and went to bed.

Next morning he called his senior servants together.

"When my lady wife returns, she is to be shown to my study to await correction."

He left the room and his valet smiled sourly.

"When he says. I would rather think if. And it ain't my lady who is needing corrective action."

There was a collective rustle as if of agreement and the servants dispersed to their duties.

Having dealt, in his own mind, with the problem of an errant wife, Cumberland returned to the pursuit of his enemy's treasure.

Some business or other dictated that Westmorland return to his family acres and Cumberland saw his opportunity to take that which he had determined to own. It was midnight when he left his house, dressed from head to toe in concealing dark clothing and with his face masked in black cloth. He took no conveyance, preferring to walk the fast-emptying streets of the city protected only by the preparedness of his physique and by the pistols he carried. Only once was he accosted, and then by a thin young prostitute who huddled in a dark doorway. He reached into a pocket and threw her a golden guinea. She caught it, and when she saw what it was her face lit until she was almost pretty.

"God bless you guv."

On another night he might have dallied awhile but his pressing need kept him moving towards another woman his mind understood to be as much a whore - even if she would undoubtedly prove more expensive than her ragged sister.

Outside a certain slim house, he stood for a long time. Hidden from view on the other side of the avenue concealed in the deep shadow between two walls, he watched as the final light went out in the servants quarters high up under the roof. When he judged everyone to be asleep he crossed the street on silent feet. The wisteria that grew up the front of the house was an easy climb and he smiled a feral smile into the darkness. The window of what he guessed must be the lady's own bedchamber was open a little, to let in, he thought, the heady scent of the purple flowers that hung about the house like bunches of grapes. Taking care to move silently he lifted the sash. This was too easy. His head and torso were in the room when something struck him on the back of the neck.

He awoke to find himself in the back of a carriage of some sort, blindfolded, and with his hands tied behind his back. The carriage drew to a halt and a pair of mercilessly strong hands lifted him. He was unceremoniously dumped on what felt like cold stone and a rough voice spoke close to his ear.

"This is your only warning. Step close to the lady again and you will not live to tell the tale."

Then he felt the sting of a sharp blade as it slashed the rope at his wrists before it caressed the skin on his face.

"Next time it's your throat."

He heard the sound of a carriage pulling away and found from somewhere the courage to fumble with the strip of fabric that covered his eyes. When he could see again he realised that he was on his own doorstep and that the wetness on his face was his own blood.

He walked into the house with all the nonchalance he could muster and it wasn't until he was safe in his own bedchamber that he allowed the shakes to overtake his body. Throwing off his clothing he dived into the whiteness of his wide bed and closed his eyes, thinking somehow to will the events of the night out of existence.

Dawn was barely breaking the morning sky when he gave up on sleep and rung for his valet. When that worthy finally appeared he resisted the temptation to throw the chamberpot and contented himself with a snarl.

"Pack my clothing and have Thunderbolt and Lightning harnessed to my curricle. I leave for Derbyshire as soon as I have broken my fast."

If his valet noticed the cut that ran from his master's cheekbone to his chin he forbore from comment, merely doing as he was bid with his thin mouth folded in a tight line.

***

Meanwhile in a grim, grey castle, perched on a crag with the North Sea crashing about its feet, Westmorland was face to face with Cumberland's wife.

"Why does he hate you so much? What did you do to him?"

"It's more what I did not do."

"What do you mean? How can you hate someone for something they did not do?"

Westmorland's large-boned and sensible wife looked up from her needlework.

"You have brothers do you not?"

"I do. But I fail to see the connection."

"Our husbands met at Eton, and Cumberland was Westmorland's fag, but, unlike many of his contemporaries, Westmorland didn't take advantage of that situation. We believe your husband felt this as rejection and that is why he hates us."

It took a moment, but when she understood that her husband's hatred stemmed from what he saw as having the first fresh buds of his love rejected by another male, Cumberland's wife's cheeks paled and she fell to the floor in a dead faint.

"Was that necessary, me dear?"

"Could you think of any other way to tell her our suspicions?"

"No. I suppose not."

He bent and lifted the fainting woman in his arms, depositing her on a convenient sofa. Then he scratched his head. His wife laughed.

"Get along with you. Let me deal with the poor despised bride."

He went, but turned on the threshold, "Do we think he has ever...?"

"I don't know and I have no intention of asking." She shooed him away.

An hour later she ran him to earth in his office. His factor was just leaving and bowed to her ladyship with unfeigned respect.

Westmorland smiled. "I don't know what this place would do without you. Nor what I would do if I am being honest."

His wife lifted one sandy brow. He coloured and shook his head.

"The women mean nothing. But..."

"But you and I were married without so much as a by-your-leave to either of us. And you elected to show your father - and mine - that you couldn't be bought, by means of the shocking career of a rakeshame."

"Only it never shocked you, did it?"

"No. It amused me. But, I think, only because I was no more enamoured of this marriage than were you. Although it has grown on me. A little."

He threw back his handsome head and laughed. Then his face changed and he looked a bit embarrassed.

"Being married to you is so comfortable. Do you never want more than comfortable companionship?"

She lifted a shoulder. "What if I said I do want more from you?"

He crossed the room to where she stood and looked down into her eyes. Although he smiled, his gaze was sombre with something vulnerable in the depths.

"Then I would try to give you what you want."

"Truly? No more opera dancers?"

"Truly. I begin to tire of the life of a fool. If you will have me, I think I would like to become a proper husband to you."

"So long as that doesn't include telling me what to do."

This time his smile reached his eyes. "Is that what a proper husband does? Because if so, I rescind my offer. I shall be an improper husband instead."

He took her hands in his and she hid her face in the white lawn of his shirt.

"We will do better," he said quietly and that felt far more important than the words they had said in a cold, dark church all those years ago.

"Yes," she agreed. "We will indeed do better. But now. Your sworn enemy and that poor shattered child he married."

"Ah yes. Him. There may be a way. My only worry is that it could break their marriage as easily as it could make it."

She lifted her eyes to his. "If it cannot be made, then it is better that she knows now while it can still be unmade."

He absorbed that idea. "Poor little creature. We'll try what we can do for her."

"Thank you. I feel such pity for her."

"But none for yourself, even though you were given in marriage to a young fool who cared not a jot."

She smiled softly. "None then. And most certainly none now. You may prove to make a damnable job of being a true husband, but I will gladly take my chances."

She left him then, pondering his options.

***

It was somewhat short of a month later and a scabrous fog blanketed the streets outside the gymnasium of one of the city's most celebrated pugilists. The great doors were barred and it would have seemed to an idle passer-by that the place was closed for the night. But, if any could have stepped inside they would have seen a very different story. The great room was ablaze with the light of hundreds of candles, but, instead of the normal baying crowd of fashionable bucks and hangers on, the room was eerily empty. All it contained, aside from the roped-off boxing ring, was a high-backed settle that obviously belonged somewhere else. The champion himself stood with one hand on the back of this seat, on which sat two obviously female figures who did not seem to be of the sort that normally haunted the rooms in pursuit of male protection. The women were both cloaked in fine wool, one wore sober grey, the other a black so lightless as to almost deceive the eye into thinking there was nobody where she sat. Their hair was hooded and each wore a dark mask concealing her face.

The champion bent forwards and spoke with careful respect. "My lady, are you sure you need to witness this? I understand the need for it to happen, but I fear that you do not understand what it is you are about to see."

The slighter of the two figures lifted a hand to adjust the blackness of her hood.

"I thank you for your concern, sir. But I have to understand for myself if I am to be mended or destroyed."

The other woman put out a grey-gloved hand. "Hush, child, let us not speak of destruction." She turned her face to the pugilist. "Is all in readiness, sir?" He nodded. "Very well, then. Let us begin."

The champion bowed very low and gave a quiet command. There was some little bustle about the roped-off arena as men brought stools and buckets of water with floating sponges to the corners of the ring. The champion stripped off his coat of superfine cloth and removed his fine lawn shirt. He handed them to a waiting servant, before vaulting the ropes and standing in the centre of the ring.

"Gentleman A," he called.

Cumberland strolled from a darkened doorway. He was stripped down to his knitted drawers and his feet were bare, but his hands were bandaged with strips of linen. His chest and arms were oiled, and shone in the candlelight, as he walked, bouncing on the balls of his feet. The woman in black twined her fingers together nervously and her companion laid a hand on top of the writhing fingers.

"Hush."

Cumberland performed a showy flip over the ropes and landed with barely a bend of his knees before recommencing his bouncing. The champion looked at him coolly and he stood still.

"Gentleman B."

Westmorland moved purposefully and with none of his opponent's studied grace, but the breadth of his shoulders and the muscular development of his chest and arms was impressive enough without theatrics.

The woman in grey drew in a ragged breath. "Mine," she breathed.

Westmorland entered the ring with practised ease and moved to stand diagonally opposite the unquiet figure of his opponent.

The champion spoke again. "Are you ready gentlemen?"

"I was born ready," Cumberland sounded both excited and dangerous. However, it was Westmorland's deep-toned "yes" that reverberated in the heads of those who watched.

The champion moved to the centre of the ring and gestured the two men forward. When they stood face to face he took a pace back.

"Begin."

Cumberland leapt forward and aimed a vicious uppercut at his opponent's square jaw. If it had made contact, it might have been a game changer. But the punch met only thin air and his forward momentum carried him onto a straight-armed jab to the solar plexus that had him gasping for breath. In a conventional prizefight his opponent would have moved in to finish the job, but Westmorland moved back and waited for him to regain his breath.

While he should, perhaps, have been grateful for such consideration, instead it made him angry and once he could breathe and see he went after the older man with every ounce of anger and pent-up frustration he had. It was a lot. However, his rage overbore the science he had learned, and his attacks, though ferocious, were ineffective - as Westmorland easily blocked or evaded his blows replying with his own stinging punches, all of which did seem to find their target. After five minutes of ineffective bullishness, Cumberland regained a measure of control and it seemed as if his skill as a boxer returned, enabling him to bully his opponent into a neutral corner. He saw his opportunity and danced in for the kill. To find himself met by a hail of punishing punches to his chest and head. Before he could readjust his mind, or his feet, a precisely judged punch took him at the point of his jaw and his legs crumpled beneath him.

As he dropped to his knees, Westmorland vaulted his kneeling figure and bore him to the ground from behind.

"Now, my friend," he said in a voice as cold as the north wind. "Now perhaps you will sit still long enough to listen when I say this game of cat and mouse is over."

Cumberland wriggled like a netted eel but Westmorland was not going to let him escape. Indeed he moved so he was astride the younger man's back.

"What do you want from me you stupid boy?"

Cumberland groaned but said nothing.

"Will you have me use you like a two penny whore? Right here and now. Will that suffice your twisted pride?"

Cumberland turned his head. "Why would I be good enough now, when I wasn't then?"

Westmorland eased the pressure on his captive's body.

"It's not a matter of 'good enough' you fool. It's simply a matter of my not having any use for boys."

Cumberland went still. "Don't lie to me."

"I don't lie. You, of all people should know that."

Westmorland stood up, and Cumberland rolled onto his back.

"What of Winchester Minor then?"

"What of him?"

"He was your bum boy for five years."

Westmorland laughed. "Only in his own little mind."

Cumberland stared into the face of the man whose betrayal of his boyhood hero worship had been the cornerstone of a wall of hatred, and he must at last have understood how it had all been built on a lie, because his cry of heart-deep pain wrenched at the gut.

Westmorland dropped to his knees to cradle his erstwhile enemy as he cried.

The slender black-clad figure made to get up from the settle, but her companion held her back.

"Leave them. They have to settle this between themselves."

"Oh. But.."

"Later."

Westmorland held out an imperious hand and one of the ring men put a bundle of clean rag in his palm. He lifted Cumberland's chin and gently cleaned the younger man's face.

"Look at you," he said kindly, "all over blood, snot and tears."

Cumberland sniffed inelegantly. "Is my nose broken?"

"Vanity, vanity." Westmorland laughed, but he gently waggled Cumberland's nose. "Well it is not wobbling, so if you can breathe through it I would suggest not. Your beauty is safe."

"Easy for you to say. I cannot think I got in above half a dozen hits on you."

"Because you allowed yourself to be angry. It was ever your downfall."

Cumberland leaned back and looked at him. "I could never make you angry, though. Could I?"

"Frequently," Westmorland laughed deep in his chest. "I'm just better at self control than you, and I was certainly not prepared to let you see how your hatred hurt me."

Cumberland absorbed this information and held out a trembling hand.

"Can you ever forgive me?"

"I think I must have already forgiven, as I let you off lightly when I might have beaten you with great severity."

"Indeed you might. I was so consumed by rage and sorrow."

"I know, and you are an idiot." Westmorland smiled, but then his face grew stern. "There is someone, though, whose forgiveness you should beg on your knees."

"Who? I owe no person…" He stopped speaking as if poleaxed. "You mean my wife?"

"I do. And before you say another word, my own wife has forgiven me my transgressions. Although I do not deserve her forgiveness."

Cumberland raised a trembling hand to his face. "I may have lost her already," he said thickly. "She left me, you know."

"I do know. But what you should know is that she came to me and begged me to help you."

"To help her?"

"No. To help you. Her heart is so great that she humbled her pride in order to try and help you."

The tears ran afresh down Cumberland's face. "Do you know where I can find her, that I may beg her forgiveness?"

"What would you have of her? You cannot ask her to forgive you if you intend to carry on humiliating her in public and threatening her in private."

Cumberland coloured the deep red of shame. "I wouldn't really have hurt her, it was just my own disgust at my behaviour being turned on her. But. How did you know?"

"My dear wife wormed the truth from her. The blow to your nose was a reminder. It was unnecessary in the context of boxing you, but I needed to make it clear how I feel about the idea that a man can beat his wife. Even if the law does allow."

Cumberland's mortification was almost a physical thing and Westmorland beckoned the black-clad woman into the ring. She came as if on wings and threw herself to her knees on the worn canvas. Taking Cumberland's shaking body into her arms she crooned soft words as if to a broken-hearted child.

Westmorland climbed out of the ring and went to where his own wife sat. She came into his arms as if it was where she had been born to be.

He smiled down at her. "I've done my best me dear. Do you think it might be enough?"

She lifted her eyes to him. "For them? I hope so. For us? Whenever I feel annoyed by you I shall think of your magnificence as you walked into the ring and my knees will turn to water and I will not be able to feel anything but unmaidenly lust."

He put his big hands around her waist and smiled the smile of the alpha predator he would always be. "Unmaidenly lust is it? We may want to talk about that."

PINK RIBBON

Maw and Paw got together because he got drunk one night and she wound up with a big belly. By the time Seth got born, the two of them had wore out the hubba hubba and were about ready to beat each other's brains to dirt. But then Paw noticed something. Maw might not be his romantic idea of a pretty little woman with a pink ribbon in her hair, but she was a mighty good farmer. And he warn't. This being how things run out, they made them a bargain and stuck to being married.

Not having been around when any of this happened, most of us kids learned about it from Grandpaw, who reckoned it was the only sensible thing Paw done in the whole of his fat, useless life.

We kids, not having a great opinion of a man what spent most of his time asleep in the sun, kinda tended to agree with him. We worked hard about the place, learning to be useful almost as soon as we could walk. Maw taught us to be farmers, and Grandpaw taught us all to read and write—which put us one step up from most of the valley kids. Paw's contribution? He'd a fine hand for the making and selling of moonshine, and that brung in enough cash money to buy us what we couldn't grow for ourselves.

About three times a year he'd load up the ole Ford truck that Seth's understanding of mechanics kept running, and the pair of them would make a moonlight run over the border to sell the booze to one of the speakeasy owners whose customers had a bottomless desire for the liquid refreshment the government declared was agin the legal law. When they went was pretty elastic—except for pig killing week when Paw'd be gone come hell or high water.

I remember asking him about it when I was no more'n a little bit of a thing. He'd just come home from a selling trip and I was sat on his lap sucking on the rare treat of a peppermint bullseye. Something about the lazy afternoon sun, made me brave enough to say the thing that was in the front of my mind.

"Paw," I says, "how comes it you ain't never here when it's pig killin' time?"

I remember, like it was yesterday, how he laughed his lazy laugh and pulled me in for a hug.

"It's the noise, kid. I can't bear the noise them hawgs make. Sounds to me like they knows their end is comin'. The way they screams, they might be humans in dying pain."

I leaned against his old check shirt and patted him with my small, dirty hand. "I guess it do sound bad. But Maw don't mind."

"No. She don't. But your maw's always been more of a farmer than me." I warn't old enough to understand the bitter edge to his voice, though I did kinda halfway think he sounded odd. I braced myself for a clip round the head but his hand on my hair was gentle so I jest cuddled in and carried on sucking my candy.

Paw leaned back in his chair and tilted his old Stetson to shade his eyes. In a very few minutes he was asleep.

It was hard winter when the twins got born, and Maw was pretty sick for a longish while. We kids kept the livestock fed and the cows milked and while the boys fed and mucked out, we girls managed the dairy and kept the house as best we could. Even Paw lent a hand here and there, so we managed.

Once Maw was well enough to take notice she spoke to each of us kids about how proud she was of our hard work. She have always been sparing of praise, and we all stood a bit taller that day. Soon after, she took the reins of the household back into her hands and Paw went back to his rocking chair and his still.

Spring come late and Maw was finally back to full health, but the winter had took a toll on her looks such as they was. She'd never been what nobody would call a beauty, but where she'd had curves before, now she was raw boned and somehow dry looking, while her long black hair was threaded with silver.

As soon as the creeks went down Paw took hisself off in the truck, but he decided to leave Seth home—which was a darn fool thing to do because Paw wouldn't have had half a clue if'n the truck broke down. Anyhow, he got away with it, and come home with a pocket full of dollars and a smile on his face.

Maw watched him a bit narrowly for a few days, but he seemed his usual lazy good-humoured self and life settled back to normal. Which was where it was when he loaded the truck again a few weeks later. He smiled into Maw's eyes.

"Them city guys is beggin' for Mountain Dew and they'll pay whatever we asks."

She lifted a shoulder and turned away, so the effort he made to kiss her goodbye missed her mouth and landed someplace about her ear.

This time he took Seth, and they was gone for better than two weeks. Maw was beginning to look pale and drawn when the sound of an engine labouring up the track let us know they was on their way home.

Me and Cletus was out front painting the porch rails so we seen her first.

Seen who?

Seen the blonde with the pink ribbons in her hair what was sat in the front of the truck beside Paw. Maw come out onto the stoop and I was watching her face when she saw the girl and put two and two together. I saw her draw in her lips and straighten her spine before she stepped forward with a smile. We didn't want to hear what they might say, so we crept out into the barn where all us kids gathered together and waited for the storm to break. Seth found us and he rubbed his hand across his chin. I can still hear the scraping sound of his hard palm against the beard he was starting to grow. His eyes were hard.

"Now I know why the dirty old dog never took me with him last time."

Cletus stood up. "What's he up to?"

"Ain't it obvious? He've gotten hisself a second wife."

You could've cut the air with a knife, as we took that in.

"Can he do that?"

"Preachers say he can. He can't marry her legal, but Maw'll have to accept her or be shunned from the church." Oldest sister, Susan, sounded tired.

Seth spat into the corner. "I guess we all have to accept her, even me."

"What'd you mean, even you?" I found my voice.

"She was my girl until she decided Paw had more to offer."

And that was how Stepmaw came into our lives. She occupied the big double bed with Paw, and Maw moved in with us girls, but outside of that she didn't seem to have much appetite for any wifely duties. She was even lazier than Paw, and the pair of them spent hours out on the porch swing smooching and giggling like as if they was both teenagers.

When she wasn't cuddling up to Paw, Stepmaw was careful to seem as sweet and girlish as her pretty clothes and the ribbons in her hair made her look. Only she couldn't quite pull it off.

It wasn't hard to see through her. We come to despise the pink ribbon she always wore in her hair, and we understood pretty well what hid behind her hard, flat eyes. She fluttered her eyelashes at the boys, while us girls got pinches and sugar-coated poison. Maybe the boys might have fell under her spell if she hadn't made her contempt for Maw so plain, but she did.

When she wasn't primping in front of the mirror, she was flirting with an unwilling Seth, treating Maw no better than some kitchen skivvy, and pouring poison into Paw's ears about fancied slights and unacceptable behaviours from us kids. We reckoned she expected Paw to take his belt to us but, besotted or not, he weren't that kind of man.

It kind of surprised us how stoopid he was where she was concerned. He never seemed to see the rat what hid under her cuddly little girl act, and she was just clever enough to keep that side under wraps when he was about.

She kept him wrapped around the pinkie finger that she never lifted to do spit for long enough that we began to think she could keep up the act forever.

Turns out she couldn't.

Harvest time come and everyone but Stepmaw was working from dawn to dusk to get in the crops. Paw rode the tractor and the rest of us pitched in wherever. By the time we were finished, Stepmaw was thoroughly bored and spiteful. We reckoned she'd take it out on Paw.

She was cleverer than that, though, instead she decided he should sell the farm and move into town.

The first we heard of it was at breakfast one morning when she put on her sweetest voice and spoke directly to Maw.

"I'm not fancying beans this morning. You reckon you could fix me some eggs?"

Maw sighed. "Whyn't you fix your own eggs?"

That set a match to Stepmaw's temper and she leaned across the table. "You should maybe treat me with more respect, otherwise what'll you and your kids do when the farm's sold and me and Ezekiel moves into town." Her voice was like the hiss of a cottonmouth snake.

The silence round the table was as thick as Maw's beans and gravy. Paw opened his mouth, but Grandpaw beat him to it.

The old man lifted his head out of his bowl. "How're you and Zeke gonna sell what don't belong to him?"

Stepmaw gave him a look that was intended to intimidate.

"You won't be here forever."

The ole man might have a neck like a turtle and only three teeth, but he've been about a while and he laughed in Stepmaw's pretty face. "I won't indeed. But who's to know if the farm'll be yours to sell when I'm gone."

He went back to his breakfast. She opened her mouth and we waited for the explosion, but calculation took over from temper and she piped down, lifting a kerchief to dab pretend tears from her eyes. Paw took his opportunity and slipped out of the back door, heading for his moonshine still in the woods. The rest of us got in with our day.

We never did quite find out what happened in the big bed that night. One thing was certain, though, Paw came to breakfast looking mulish and Stepmaw was even more sour-mouthed than usual. We kinda reckoned she was determined to break him to harness, not understanding how stubborn a weak man can be if you back him into a corner. Paw even started talking to Maw again, though that made Stepmaw even harsher and more spiteful the minute his back was turned. Things carried on pretty much the same for a couple weeks and we was beginning to hope Paw'd get tired of his pretty doll once he admitted she warn't what she seemed. It might even have happened except that Stepmaw come to her senses and put her mind to bringing Paw back around her finger. She apologised to Maw in her best little girl voice, and she started spending time talking to Grandpaw as he sat in his chair of an evening. He didn't seem too impressed, and Maw certainly wasn't. However, Paw bought it hook, line and sinker and he smiled mistily when he looked at her in her pretty gingham dresses with the bright ribbons tying up her yellow hair.

So it was that he was pretty much back where she wanted him to be when pig killin' came along.

So far as we knew, Stepmaw planned to ride along with Paw and Seth, but the whole house heard the blow-up the night before they was due to go. First we heard he was shouting like we never heard him do before or since and her cryin' and carryin' on in the background.

Then we hears the sound of a slap followed by other sounds we wasn't so keen on listening to. Sister Susan looked grim.

"She always got that when she wants to bring him to heel."

"Got what?" That was six-year-old Bessie.

"Never you mind."

Next morning, breakfast was before sunup and Maw dished up a mess of beans and bacon thick enough to line a man's stomach. Stepmaw never appeared and nobody cared enough to ask. Paw looked grim, but Maw pretended not to notice, kissing him goodbye and telling him to be careful.

The truck bumped off down the track and Maw smiled a cold, secret little smile.

About lunchtime Stepmaw come into the kitchen all dressed in her best.

"Where's Ezekiel?"

"Gone to town."

Stepmaw's mouth fell open, then she closed it with a snap. I thought we was in for it, but Maw set her jaw and even Stepmaw wasn't darn fool enough to take on Maw when she looked like that.

Stepmaw took herself back to bed for a good sulk and Maw got down to work. The rest of us managed the farm and the house while Maw shut herself in the old dairy and got on with the killing and butchering.

I kept myself to the kitchen while the killing was going on. I always think of what Paw said about the screams of the dying pigs and how human they sound so I stop where I can hear them least.

Wasn't until two days after Paw left that anybody thought to look for Stepmaw. Sister Susan got that duty, being big enough that Stepmaw never pinched or slapped her. She come back to the kitchen looking puzzled.

"Durn fool woman ain't there?"

"How'd you mean ain't there?" Maw didn't sound as if she cared too much.

"Just ain't there. The room's empty."

Grandpaw grinned. "I don't reckon nobody will miss her."

"We won't, but where can she have gone?" One of the little ones asked.

"Probably hiked down to the highway, riding her thumb into town to catch up with Paw and see if she can't persuade him to spend some money on her."

Maw lifted a shoulder. "Likely. Young Zeke, you better take the dawgs and see if you can find any trace of her in the woods."

He groaned.

"I know it's a waste of time, but your Paw would never forgive us if'n she was laying someplace injured."

"Okay Maw."

Young Zeke and Paw's coon hounds done a thorough search of the woods. The only place they found any trace of Stepmaw was on the track down to the highway, which made us think she must have gone after Paw like we guessed.

Three days later, we hears the truck labouring up the hill and most of us finds a place to watch from—wanting to hear Maw give Stepmaw a piece of her mind for running off and wasting a day of Young Zeke's time. Only she ain't in the truck. It's only Paw and Seth.

Maw went to the driver's window and had some words with Paw, who got out of the truck and motioned Seth to take it round to the barn. He and Maw went into the parlour and shut the door.

We never heard no shouting, so we all went about our work, meeting up when Maw beat on the old tin tray to call us in for dinner.

We always have a slap-up spread when Paw comes home after pig killin', but this year Maw outdone herself. Everyone had a special pie with their name pricked in the golden crust. The pies was piping hot and oozing gravy and we all set to with a will. For a goodish while there wasn't a sound to be heard except the scrape of knives and forks on plates and rhythmic chomping.

All of a sudden Paw gives a cry like you never want to hear in your life. It seemed to me to be made up of pain and fear and something else I couldn't understand. He pushed his plate away and ran out into the dooryard, where we could hear the sounds of him throwing up his guts on the ground. Maw picked up his plate and scraped its contents into the dawgs' trough. They fell on it, snapping and snarling, and it was soon all gone.

Maw smiled a closed-mouth smile and rubbed her palms together as if she'd just finished a dirty job. All around the table there was noise and chatter, as the family tried to figure out what had happened to Paw.

I sat silent because I knew. I was sat right beside Paw and I seen him fork a choice lump of meat and find a scrap of pink ribbon floating in his gravy…

HANGING ON THE MOON

Beth and Peter had been friends as children, and sweethearts as teenagers, so it was no surprise that they married before his call up took him away to war.

On the night before he went, they sat late in the orchard under a big fat moon. If Beth cried a little that was nobody's business but their own, and neither was the cementing of their love in the kindly silver light. In the end, though, her abiding memory of that night would be the sight of him swinging across the face of the moon on the old rope swing.

"I'll make you a promise, love," he cried, "when this is all over we'll come back here and swing in the moonlight."

But then morning came and he had to go. Leaving her to manage as best she could without him.

Work helped. The physical labour of keeping the farm going without the young men left her tired enough not to cry in her lonely bed. Just as she had managed to believe she had got used to him being gone, she discovered he hadn't left her alone. She was pregnant. For a while she told nobody, save her silent giant of a father who smiled the smile that wrinkled his brown face and made sure she didn't overwork herself. It was winter when she started to show, and on a bright Sunday morning she walked the three miles to where Peter's mother lived bearing the news of her pregnancy.

It was difficult, because Peter's mother didn't care for Beth, and the loss of her husband in the last war had convinced her that her son would never return from this one. An exhausted Beth turned her face to the long walk home to find her father waiting at the crossroads with a tidy cob harnessed to the gig that hadn't seen use since his wife had died.

"Get you up," he said, "talking to the sorrowful widow is some hard."

For a while they were quiet, but they began to talk over the day-to-day business of the farm and by the time they were home Beth felt herself settled.

"Thanks Dad."

He said nothing until later that night as they sat beside the fire hooking a rag rug.

"I think you know I wasn't keen on you marrying Peter."

"I did know it, and I wondered why."

"It isn't the lad, it's his mother. She'll make mischief if she can."

Beth looked down at her own busy hands. "Aye. But I can't worry about her."

Dad smiled.

Beth had an easy pregnancy, and when the lilac was scenting her mother's garden she gave birth to a daughter. She wanted to call her Petra for her father, but he had other ideas, writing that he would have his daughter called Rose for Beth's mother.

Rose it was, and the quiet christening was marred only by the sourness of the baby's grandmother.

Summer was almost over when Peter got embarkation leave before heading for the jungles of Burma. Beth drove to the station to meet him, and was pleased to see he looked brown and fit, if less heedless than the boy who went away a year ago. Outside his mother's cottage she drew to halt.

"Go in. I'll feed Rose."

He jumped down. Beth had barely settled her daughter to her breast when he came back with a face like thunder. She handed him the reins and hoped he wouldn't overturn them in a ditch. But she did him a disservice, as he drove carefully even though the set of his jaw spoke of extreme anger.

They were about halfway home before he spoke.

"You know what the old bitch is saying?"

"No."

"She tells me 'everybody' knows Rose isn't mine."

Beth grimace. "I don't care about 'everybody'. But I do care about you. Who do you think fathered Rose?"

He drew the gig to a halt. "I don't think, love, I know. Rose is my daughter. I fancy she was conceived on that last night in the orchard."

"That's all right then."

He briefly nuzzled the top of her breast beside Rose's downy head then shook the reins. The patient cob plodded onwards as his passengers fought their way back to peace and tranquillity.

At the farm, Dad took a look at Peter's face.

"Been to see your ma?"

Beth could hear the anger under his calm.

"I have. And it'll likely be the last time."

Beth handed Rose to Dad and jumped down.

"Go and stable the cob. I'll get the kettle on."

By the time the men came inside, the baby was asleep in her cradle and the tea was brewed. They sat down together, and it was as if Peter had never been away. For all his mother's airs and graces, he was a farmer at heart. He spent the best part of his five days working side by side with his father-in-law but the nights were for Beth in their big white bed.

Page 28

On his last night at home, some benevolent god dictated a big, white moon in a cloudless sky. Dad looked up from his end of the rag rug.

"I can watch Rose if you two want to go and look at the moon."

Beth blushed, but Peter grabbed her hand and dragged her out into the sweetness of the night. Much later, she watched him swing across the moon.

"Next time I swing like this let's hope this cruel war is over."

Beth quietly stored up memories of the enchanted night.

Two years passed quietly, until the day Beth was in the dairy churning butter and singing a little song to a sleepy toddler. Dad came in with a buff envelope in his hand. Beth kept on churning.

"Will you open it? I don't think I can."

Did slit the envelope.

"Peter is missing. Believed captured."

Beth felt the blood leave her face, but the butter was about to turn so she concentrated on the practicalities rather than thinking about the words. He said no more, simply picking up his granddaughter and striding out of the dairy. When he and Rose returned from their expedition, Beth was in the kitchen. She looked up and tried for a smile.

"All we can do," she said in a cracked little voice, "is wait, and hope, and pray. And tell his mother..."

If Beth cried in her bed at night she showed a brave face in the light of day, as she soldiered on as much a casualty of the war as anyone on the frontline.

She had all but given up hope when the postman cycled up the farm track bearing yet another telegram. Dad opened the envelope.

"Peter's alive, love. Crawled out of the jungle with one of his mates on his back..."

There was something in his voice that made Beth grab a hold of a chair for support.

"But?'

"But they had to amputate his left leg just below the knee."

Beth closed her eyes.

The next news came in a letter from Peter himself. He spoke of relief at finding himself alive, and of love for Beth and Rose. But then he asked for the hardest thing Beth could imagine. He begged her to not come to the hospital, where he was being fitted with an artificial leg and taught to walk again. Instead he asked her to wait for him on the farm. As the hot tears scalded her throat, Dad came to her rescue.

"Let him have his pride Beth. It's maybe all this war has left to him."

Beth could see that, so she wrote that she would wait forever if that was what he needed.

She waited, counting the days, until he wrote that he was coming home 'tin leg and all'.

Leaving Rose with Dad, Beth drove to the station. When the train puffed in, her eyes scanned the platform. For a moment she thought he wasn't there. But then she saw him. His head bobbed up and down oddly as he walked, but he was walking and he was carrying his kitbag like it weighed nothing. She found herself unable to move or speak. But he understood, throwing his bag into the gig and heaving himself up beside her. He took the reins from her unresisting hands and clicked his tongue at the patient cob in the shafts. Once they were away from prying eyes he stopped the gig.

"Are you real, love?"

"Real enough to be wanting you in my arms in our bed."

Which was all the reassurance she needed. They talked in quiet happiness, until the grey chimneys of his mother's cottage came into view.

"Shall we stop?"

"No. I have to see her. But not today. Today is for us."

But Beth put a hand on his wrist. "She needs to see you."

He blinked. "You're a wonder to me, you are. She wouldn't care about you."

"That don't matter I have so much, and she has so little. You go in."

He drew the gig to a halt. "I'll not be long."

He was true to his word, but the surprise was that his mother came with him. She peered up to where Beth sat in the gig.

"Thank you."

Beth didn't have the heart to be anything but kind so she smiled. "Will you come for your dinner on Sunday?"

"Yes please. I'd like that." She kissed Peter on the cheek before running indoors.

Peter clambered back into the gig and Beth leaned against him.

"I'm glad you went in. I've felt sorry for the silly old besom for a long time, but I never had what she needed. Until now.'

He shook the reins and they went home, where Dad and Rose waited.

The joyousness of that day is hard to write. Peter and Dad thumped each other's shoulders. Rose decided to flirt with this stranger. And Beth drank in the ordinary in the face of extraordinary joy.

With supper eaten Peter stumped over to the window.

"Seems as if the moon has come out to welcome me home..."

It wasn't the same as before, because this time Beth wasn't being dragged into the orchard by an impulsive boy, she was walking carefully hand-in-hand with a man who had survived to come home to her.

Later, as the moon rose higher she lay in the grass watching Peter's efforts at swinging. It was hard to get the rhythm, although he made it eventually and as she watched him swing across the moon Beth knew there would be challenges ahead, but she also knew her heart had found its safe harbour in the hands of the boy who had become a man.

Officer Connolly was neither young nor new to the job, but this sort of thing was never pleasant and he hunched his shoulders in his blue uniform coat as he knocked on the blue-painted door. The outside light came on and a thin young woman with a child on her hip opened the door. She saw his uniform and sighed.

"What's he done now?"

The girl sounded almost unbearably weary and Connolly felt the stirring of unusual pity.

" Mrs Jackson?"

The girl laughed, but it was a harsh sound like scraping fingernails down a chalkboard.

" No. But I'm Donny Jackson's woman and this is his daughter."

" Then I'm sorry to have to inform you that there was a road traffic accident on the ring road this afternoon, in which a town car was comprehensively crushed by a thirty-ton lorry. Your man was a passenger in the town car." He broke off, looking, had he known it, greenish-pale and sick. " Look. There wasn't enough left of him to identify in the normal way, but we found CCTV footage from the town centre that shows Donny Jackson getting into the car outside Jake's billiards hall. Also, whoever was in the passenger seat of the crushed car was wearing Donny's watch and his Saint Christopher medallion."

The girl's face was by now paper white under her tan and she swayed slightly on her feet. For a moment the policeman thought she was going to faint, but instead she grasped the edge of the door.

" Thank you for coming to tell me."

She closed the door gently, and as the uniformed constable turned away he could hear the heartbreaking sound of her sobs. That depth of sorrow woke something in his cicatrised heart, and, as he walked away, he thought he would come back in a few days. Just to see how things were.

Three days later, and it was his day off so he wasn't in uniform when he knocked. The girl opened the door cautiously, as she obviously didn't recognise him. He made her understand who he was, and that he had come to assure himself of her welfare, so she let him in. To his surprise the room was filled with cardboard boxes.

"If you'd come tomorrow you wouldn't have found us here," she explained. "The house belongs to Donny's mam and she's kicking us out."

He was shocked, if unsurprised, at such callous behaviour.

"Where will you go?"

"Back to my own mam. I've nowhere else."

"Hang on a minute. Let me make a phone call."

He got the girl, whose name turned out to be Betty, and her child into a flat by the river, courtesy of the company whose lorry had effectively minced little Donna's father.

Having somehow made himself responsible for Betty and Donna, it became second nature to call on them daily, and make sure they got whatever was due to them - as opposed to the crumbs that Donny's family thought they might be able to spare.

With enough to eat, and no worries about illegal activities or hard men in suits with shooters, Betty put on a little weight and the prettiness that had attracted Donny began to show itself again. She started to sing as she cleaned her little home and the dimple in her left cheek danced when she smiled.

Donny died on a filthy November afternoon, and, to give him his due, it wasn't until Easter that a certain burly red-haired policeman moved himself into Betty's flat and her bed.

Jim Connolly wasn't a bad sort of a man and Betty was happier and better cared for than she had ever been before. If a corner of her heart would always belong to Donny Jackson, she certainly never said anything to Jim about it.

They settled down happily enough, and Jim began to look forward to coming home to a cooked tea on the table and Donna's innocent chatter about her day. He also, when he thought about it for long enough to admit it to himself, understood that Betty's smiles were becoming the underpinnings of his life.

In the middle of August, Betty fainted while she was dishing up his tea. He rushed her to the doctor only to find out he was going to be a father.

"Well, that settles that doesn't it. I was going to wait a while, but we'll be married as soon as the banns are read."

Betty looked at him open mouthed. "You sure Jim?"

"I am and I'll be adopting Donna too."

Understanding this to be as close to a declaration of love as Jim could ever come, Betty smiled and nodded.

Jim Connolly junior was a big, bouncing redhead of a baby, and seemed quite well aware of his status at the centre of the universe. Even his father would lean over the cradle when nobody was about and touch a huge finger to the baby's soft cheek.

The family moved from the flat to a house with its own little garden when Baby Jim was a year old and Betty was already thickening with his brother or sister.

It was a hot, stuffy afternoon, a couple of weeks after the move and Betty was taking the kids to the park, via a visit to Donny's mam. She turned the corner into the street where Donny's family lived, and

Mrs J came out of her house to see her granddaughter. She hugged the little girl and grinned at Betty.

"I shouldn't ought to say this," the old woman rasped in her tobacco-roughened voice, "but I reckon our Donny done you a favour when he got hisself squashed."

Betty patted her arm. "Maybe so. But we miss him don't we."

Mrs J wiped a furtive tear. "Yes. The bugger was the apple of my eye. And he knew it. Thanks for letting me see little Donna, she's all I have of him."

"Aye. I know that, and you're all she has of him too."

They didn't stay much longer, as the coolness of the park beckoned. Betty sat on a convenient bench, while Donna clambered monkey-like about the tall climbing frame. Once she was sure the little girl was safely occupied, Betty let her mind wander a little - remembering how Donny's mam had never had any time for her while he was alive, and the callous way the old woman had driven her from the mean little house she and Donny had shared right after he was killed. None of that had been unexpected, but when Mrs J had humbled her pride enough to come to the flat and beg to be allowed to see Donna that had been a surprise. It had never occurred to her to say no, and when the old woman had gone on her way she also remembered the warmth of Jim's arm about her and how his approval had made her feel. He had kissed her on the top of her head and spoken in a slightly thickened voice.

"You're some kind of a girl, Betty. Did it never occur to you that you could have said no?"

She had looked up at him in some confusion. "Why'd I want to do that? It ain't her fault she's the way she is, and Donna's her only grandbaby."

The thumbs he rubbed across her cheekbones had felt like a blessing of sorts.

The next day he brought her flowers, yellow scented roses and oxeye daisies tied with a bow of yellow ribbon. If she concentrated she could still smell those roses.

But that was then, and now it was time to go home and water the garden before she cooked fish and chips for tea. She scooped up Donna and sat the tired little girl in the end of the pram, where she started up a soft-voiced babble of conversation with her baby brother. They were all but home when a pair of figures in a bus stop caught her eye. They seemed incongruous in this settled family area although she couldn't at first figure out why. The woman fitted in fine, being young and very modestly dressed with her mouse-brown hair coiled in a neat bun and a blue linen hat to shield her from the afternoon sun. No. It was the man who was wrong. He had his back to her, but his pinstripe suit, patent leather shoes and fedora hat marked him as a wide boy to anyone with eyes to see. Then he turned around and her heart did strange things in her chest. It was Donny. He recognised her almost immediately and the smile that lifted one corner of his mouth took her back to the dancehall where they first met. He winked, and bent his head to the girl in the bus shelter.

As the girl lifted her hand Betty could see the gold of a wedding ring. She looked down at the band on her own left hand and that steadied her more than anything else could have. While Donny pitched his new love whatever tale he was weaving, Donna looked up at Betty and grinned.

"Hungry Mum," she said.

And those simple words solidified something in Betty's chest, showing her precisely what she needed to do. Donny Jackson had walked away from his life, his debts, his enemies, and his responsibilities. Now, if she wasn't mistaken, he was thinking he could pick up where he left off. Only he couldn't. His face might still be able to set her stomach aflutter, but she couldn't forgive what he had done. Not only had he left her with nothing, he had also left his mother to mourn him as dead. Worst of all, though, there was Donna, and without Jim that little girl would have been going to bed hungry at least five nights out of seven.

Betty stiffened her spine and watched Donny come out of the bus shelter walking with his usual swagger. He walked towards her with his hands outstretched and she blanked him, willing her eyes to show no sign of recognition. She drew almost level with him and he opened his mouth to speak. Betty ran the wheels of the pram over his highly polished shoes and then kept on walking.

ROUGH MUSIC

As night blanketed the sky with navy blue shot with stars, the tawdry daytime atmosphere of the fairground changed, becoming imbued with brightly suggestive glamour.

Families took their children home to bed, while the stamped earth between the rides and sideshows became the province of groups of teenage girls redolent of chainstore perfume and the packs of young men who preyed on them.

The waltzers and dodgems saw pinkly excited young women pressing coins into the hands of dark young men with tattoos who smelled faintly of diesel and danger. And all the time the local lads circled, looking out of the corners of their eyes at the sultry beauties who sold candy floss and invited the unwary to try their hand at the coconut shy or the rifle range. The biggest and bravest of the farm boys were already halfway drunk on rough cider and their own manliness and the inevitability of a fight to end the night only served to add piquancy to the mix.

The girl who walked quietly towards the sound of roaring engines inside the high perimeter of the wall of death looked somehow out of place in the hurly burly. She was pretty enough in a brown-skinned and fresh faced way, but her clothes were a little more modest than those of her sisters and she seemed deaf to the blandishments of the hawkers around her.

At the gate she paid her shilling and climbed to the very highest bank of seats from where she could watch the muscular ballet of the swooping motorcycles.

She felt someone come and sit behind her and an unfamiliar voice spoke close to her ear.

"What's a pretty girl like you doing all alone on a Saturday night?"

"Watching the bikes." She didn't even turn her head.

He subsided, but didn't move. Neither spoke until the show finished and the two riders removed their helmets and bowed to the four compass points. The girl watched the older of the two with fierce concentration.

"What'r you looking at him for. He's old enough to be your father. And anyway he has odd eyes."

"Old enough to be my father is he?" There seemed to be a joke there and the young man felt excluded. He put a hand under her chin and turned her face towards him. The eyes that regarded him in mild surprise were mismatched: one summer blue and one dark brown.

While he was working his head around that, she walked out of the booth leaving the fairground behind.

Stopping in the rather neglected churchyard she bent to put her crumpled wall of death ticket on a newish grave.

"Now I see how it was mum. Rest in peace."

She touched the letters sharply incised in the headstone before turning away and getting on with her life.

BIG ORANGE AND THE MAMBO WOMAN

It was always kinda weird in the aquarium, and nowhere was weirder than the octopus tank. People brought stuff and put it in the water, just to see how Big Orange reacted. Maria stood in the knee-deep mist and watched him sidle over to the strange statue the fat woman in Bermuda shorts had lowered into the water. She could tell - by the way the woman, and the group of people she came with, stared into the cool clear water - that this reaction was even more important than usual. And she was pretty sure it wasn't going to end well.

It didn't. Big Orange reared up and smashed the flimsy thing with one swipe of his massive tentacles. Then he moved away.

The fat woman spoke. "I guess that tells us then don't it..."

One by one her companions nodded and as they filed out of the aquarium Maria got the feeling some sort of secret pact had been signed. For a moment she shivered, then she forgot the woman as Big Orange came to the glass to stare out at her with his impenetrable eyes.

"Why you smash the thing, big boy?" she asked idly. She almost fell to the ground when she felt his response like a wave of the salty water in his tank.

"Bad thing. Voodoo thing."

Maria swallowed the bile that rose in her throat, but she was made of stern stuff and knew what to do about voodoo bitches on her patch.

"Okay, big guy, leave it me."

The octopus regarded her pleadingly before dropping to the bottom of the tank and pulling his weedy nest tight about him. Maria dragged herself away and hurried about Big Orange's business with her sandals slapping on the damp tiles. First she went to the keepers' lodge.

"Broken crockery in da big orange man tank. Some crazies been throw a muppet in dere."

"Dios Maria. You go for get a mambo..."

"I goin' man."

But first she had to beard the Director in his den. She tapped briefly on his office door.

"Come."

She poked her head into the room, meeting the icy blue eyes of Doctor Magnus Thorssen. He was a tall, thin Swede who was noted for his acid tongue and his lack of respect for local traditions. Many of the local girls sighed after his chiselled cheekbones and sea blue eyes. Maria, who would have been ashamed to her bones to run after a broni, wouldn't even admit to herself how this man made the blood sing in her veins - even if he did have a stick so far up his ass it shoulda come out of the top of his neatly barbered head.

"Trouble in octopus tank. People thrown bad stuff in there. I be going for help."

Then she shut the door and ran before she could be caught drooling.

Maria went as fast as her sandalled feet would take her to the snug little home of her mother's sister. She tapped respectfully on the door.

"Who that?"

"Is Maria, tia Benita. There be trouble at the aquarium. Big Orange smells bokor magic."

"You sure chile?"

"I am."

"Then I's coming."

Benita was not at all what popular imagination thinks of a voodoo mambo as being - she was far from skinny, had all her own hair, and didn't mumble one bit. She was, in fact, a tall handsome woman of some fifty summers with a round good natured face and a lot of gold teeth. She smiled easily, but right now looked far from pleased. She swept out of her house, followed by a positive river of acolytes carrying gourds and pouches and all manner of arcane goods.

"Maria. You just come along us now."

As one person the acolytes glared at Maria, who laughed at their jealous malice, but Benita turned a wrathful face on them.

"Anybody wants to be questioning my decisions, now would be a good time to run..."

The sulky ones subsided and the whole group made good speed to the back entrance of the aquarium, where the director awaited them. Maria worried that he was there to bar their entry, but he actually held out his hands in welcome.

"My thanks. I don't know what has been happening, but I do know that the air in here tastes bad and smells foul. And the pieces of pottery the keepers are pulling out of the cephalopod pool make my hair stand on end."

Benita pursed her lips in thought. "That don't be good. You gonna need to close off the area."

"Done already."

The scientist and the voodoo woman eyed each other in silence for a moment, but the quiet was far from confrontational. In the end Benita spoke.

"How brave you be, skinny white guy?"

"Honestly, I don't know. But this place is in my care so I will stand up to be counted."

"That be good enough." She turned a jaundiced eye on the small crowd that had already formed and addressed her acolytes firmly. "I gonna open da portal. You lot to guard. Nothin' comes in. But I be sending stuff out. You gets that."

The young ones nodded.

"Maria. You gets to go in the water with the big guy."

Maria swallowed, but accepted her aunt's words.

"Skinny white guy, you is with me."

It didn't take long for things to get arranged to Benita's satisfaction.

With a portal to who knew where open and a ring of chanting acolytes around it, Benita signalled to Maria and grasped Magnus by his thin hand. Maria pulled the mask over her face and dropped gently into the tank. It creeped her out bit when the giant cephalopod crept out of his bed and wrapped his tentacles gently around her body. She had seldom been so thankful for a wetsuit in her life, but she steeled herself to pat the creature on one of his sinewy 'arms'. He made a small mewing noise and Maria felt pity for him.

"It's okay, boy. Tia Benita is here. She gonna send dat bad magic right back where it belong."

She made the thought as strong and positive as she could, and the creature relaxed a little.

The first awareness of anything happening came with a strange vibration in the water, it was disturbingly just off-kilter enough that the human mind couldn't catch the rhythm. It made Maria feel nauseated and Big Orange cringed as he curled himself tighter around her. Maria found herself stroking him as if he was a crying child.

"You hushabye now. Tia Benita not gonna let no bad happen to you."

The vibration stopped, and even through the water Maria could hear the mambo singing in her strong contralto voice. As she sang, bits and pieces of something floated to the top of the pool, where the bravest of the maintenance guys appeared to be collecting them in a piece of fine white cloth. The water around Maria and Big Orange started to heat up, but Tia Benita was having none of that and she spoke a word of so much power that the panes of glass in the roof high above the octopus tank rang like bells.

Maria was beginning to think this was going to be a straightforward clearance job when the sand in the bottom of the tank started to move. It circled on itself like a maelstrom of yellow particles, and then it became a pillar of spiralling sand. When it reached the surface of the water a creature shouldered itself out of the whirlpool to stand on the surface of the water.

"Hey, mambo woman," it called derisively, "you think you big enough to content with PaPa himself."

"You ain't no PaPa. Fact you ain't even a pup. You gonna go back aisy or do I gonna hafta send you."

The creature on the water swelled indignantly. Once again, Maria felt heat, but it was quickly quenched. And then a very strange thing happened. Big Orange grasped her in his tentacles and rose to the surface right beside the hulking figure that must have been the soul of the muppet that the strange crew threw into the water. The dark thing looked at the huge octopus out of deep-set red eyes.

"This ain't your fight sea monster."

Big Orange swelled his chest and began to sing, with Tia Benita and her acolytes joining in immediately. As the song swelled Magnus stepped forward.

"By the spirit of my Viking ancestors I bid you return from whence you came. Lest all of Valhal come forth and punish thee for thy transgression."

The creature made as if to sneer, but even as it curled its lip the skinny director swelled to an immensity to match the dark soul. The northman's shoulders were like those of an ox and his huge hands swung a war axe as if it was no more than a blade of grass. His piercing blue gaze bored into the red depths of the eyes of his adversary and he laughed a deep and booming laugh.

"Leave now, little draugr (demon). Leave and fight another day or meet dauða bræðrumaður (death bringer) here and now."

The dark thing licked it's lips with a thick, red tongue. "I will leave. But I was summoned and I am owed a life."

Tia Benita laughed, although it was the sort of a sound that bodes ill for somebody. She crooked a finger and almost at once the air thickened while the sound of cursing bounced off the water like waves of foul-smelling bodily fluid.

The dark thing rolled back its lips in an approximation of a smile, before eying Maria in a fashion she found disturbing. She wasn't Benita's niece for nothing, though. She raised her hands and concentrated briefly. The muppet that appeared in her hands was a tiny, perfect version of the dark creature. The summoning snarled at Maria and the muppet grew hot in her fingers.

"Stop that," she said firmly, and showed it the hat pin she held in her other hand. The muppet cooled. "Behave yourself and you shall take this with you. Anger me and I will keep my hand about your heart forever."

Magnus laughed deep in his chest. "We may want to talk when all this is over."

"We may," Maria replied primly.

Whatever they may have been going to say next was interrupted by the arrival of a woman Maria recognised as being the one who dropped the simulacrum into the water. Big Orange made a sound that would have been a snarl in a creature that possessed that sort of a throat. The woman saw who had summoned her and made to move on Tia Benita with her hands clawed. She didn't get to within twenty feet, however, because the dark entity reached across and grasped her by the throat.

"How dare you touch me Giglamel. I made you," she hissed, "and I can unmake you just as easy".

"I think not. I think you stole me. Dragged me screaming from the place where I belong. Enslaved me. Held my soul in a pot." The creature shook her like she was a rag. "Now you owe me."

It bent and rolled back its lips before biting the fat woman's neck. Maria could see its throat work as it swallowed the blood that would bind the woman to its will. After a moment it lifted its head and let the woman go. She ran, but she would now go only where the creature allowed her to.

It laughed harshly, showing bloodstained teeth, before bowing and holding a hand out to Maria. She shook her head.

"Oh no, my friend. Not until you are actually leaving."

It made a grab. But Maria was watching for the move and stepped back. The dark entity snarled and snaked its hand towards her unprotected throat. But she stabbed its groping hand with the hatpin. It screamed, high and thin, and brought its injured hand to its mouth, before beginning to spin widdershins. Faster and faster and faster it spun and when it slowly descended into the vortex Maria threw the muppet in after it.

For a few seconds disembodied and guttural laughter filled the air then it was gone, and the atmosphere felt fresh and clean again.

Big Orange uncurled himself from around Maria's body and slowly descended to the bottom of his pool. Tia Benita smiled at her niece.

"Well done chile. You go get outta that suit while I seals up the portal."

Maria scuttled off, returning a few minutes later to find the skylights open and the aquarium filled with calm, clear, fresh air. Tia Benita and Magnus Thorssen, who had returned to his thin severe self, stood in quiet conversation. Maria breathed in the vague scent of ozone and grinned at her aunt.

"Thanks, Tia Benita. You sorted that thing good."

"Not without help, chile. Not without help. You done proper. I been proud of you."

Maria felt the blush start at her neck. Magnus laughed, but it was a kindly sound.

"It has been an odd sort of an afternoon," he spoke in his normal precise tones, with nothing about him seeming to connect to the giant berserker he had become when face to face with the dark creature.

Maria was a little saddened by the return of the dry, cold scientist, and more than a little surprised when he took her hand and raised it to his lips. Startled, she looked up into his eyes to see them as blue as the sea and warm with approval. When he let go of her hand, he sighed.

"I am just discovering ," he said carefully, "that we are not always precisely what we seem. Not even myself."

"Least of all yourself, Doctor Thorssen."

"I think we have seen too much this day for Doctor Thorssen to be appropriate. My name is Magnus."

Maria chewed that one over in her mind for a moment, then thought 'what the hell'.

She dropped him half an ironic curtsey. "Pleased to meet you Magnus."

Tia Benita laughed, richly amused by a joke neither Maria nor Magnus could see. She waved one large hand at her train of trainees who dispersed at a gallop, before shaking hands with Magnus and kissing Maria on both cheeks. She looked at the tall Swede in some disapproval.

"You need to get some meat on them there bones."

Then she was gone, leaving nothing behind her but the smell of the sea.

Magnus smiled down at Maria and offered a hand. She put her own hand in his and they left the building together. Neither spoke until they were walking down the dusty little road that led to the beach. Magnus opened and shut his mouth a bit and it came to Maria that he was actually shy. That made her feel braver.

"I could use a big drink and a bowl of gumbo."

"I also. But the places I have found to eat are not very..."

"You just come with me."

She felt a little like a bustling tugboat with a tall ship in tow, but he followed obediently.

Benny's Bar was hidden from the eyes of the day trippers and holidaymakers, and it had obviously passed Magnus by too. He looked a bit out of place among the compact little island men and their broad-beamed women, but he sat where Maria pointed and when she put a bowl of steaming gumbo and a can of Red Stripe in front of him he grinned like a schoolboy and set to.

Maria felt somehow comforted by his enthusiasm for the homely things she could offer. Just maybe he wasn't such a stuffed shirt after all - even when he wasn't waving a war axe and talking old Norse.

A lot of food and a good dollop of rum later they were walking along a deserted stretch of beach with a pink moon hanging in the navy blue sky above them.

"I think we must talk about today," Magnus said abruptly. "About what I became in my anger."

Maria understood that he was deeply disturbed by the thought that a Viking berserker hid inside his dryly intellectual exterior. She looked at the hard lines of his face in the moonlight.

"You ain't the only one surprised yourself. I never made no muppet before. And I shouldn't know how. I guess we both done what was needful." He still looked doubtful and she sought to reassure him. "I rather liked your Viking."

"You did. You were not disgusted?"

"No. Though I do wonder what you are doing here with me."

Magnus didn't answer and Maria thought she'd blown it, so she stared down at their two sets of feet in the white sand. His were long and bony and almost as pale as the sand while her own were square and brown and plumply fleshed. He followed the direction of her gaze.

"We do not match well. And yet we walk together in harmony."

"Only because you shorten your stride to let me keep up."

He touched her face and she found herself all but drowned in the icy blueness of his eyes. She flinched, suddenly afraid of the attraction she felt to one so far above her in status and wealth. He felt her involuntary movement, but put it down to another reason altogether.

"I know I am pale and soberly unexciting. Even with the berserker lurking under the skin. I know this and I think myself to be a poor mate for you. But I would try if you will have me."

Maria didn't know what to say, but she knew this was her only chance if she wanted this man in her life so she pulled on his hand and brought him to a halt.

"Oh man," she whispered, "I ain't never wanted nothing like I want you."

And, as it turned out, that was enough. The laughing devils were back in his eyes and he tumbled her to the soft sand kissing her for the first time - while his hands...

A long time later he put a palm on either side of her face "ek elska þik (I love you)", he said.

Not so far away a plump mambo woman showed her gold teeth in a happy grin.

"And done," she said.

In the very centre of the aquarium a huge orange cephalopod smiled an octopus smile before settling in his seaweedy bed.

ONE WEEK…

At the time it hadn't seemed like too much to barter with the little man with the domed skull who had offered a solution to her predicament. At first he had asked for her virginity as a downpayment, but when she laughed and pointed out that it was a rose that had been plucked a good while since he had pushed out his long upper lip and made an old-maidish tisking noise. But then he had brightened. His master, he said, would be content with a week of her company in recompense for helping her out. At a time convenient to her, of course.

She had agreed hastily, frankly in so much fear of the consequences of her actions that she would have agreed to anything he suggested. Now, however, with the threat of prison no longer hanging over her head, she would have dearly loved to wriggle out of the deal, but there seemed to be no escape.

It was, therefore, with a fairly bad grace that she boarded the Eurostar for Brussels on a freezing cold Sunday afternoon in the pouring rain.

"Belgium…" she mused inwardly, "who lives in Belgium?"

That was a question that she was never to have answered. A pressed and barbered chauffeur, carrying a huge umbrella, met her on the station concourse and escorted her to a waiting limousine. He tenderly helped her into the rear of the vehicle.

"Our journey will be of about four hours duration, madam."

She nodded as regally as she could, whilst mentally trying to pin down his middle European accent.

He got into the driver's seat and the vehicle moved away as smoothly as if it ran on ball bearings. The sound of the doors locking was almost shockingly loud. She reminded herself that her own more modest saloon car performed precisely the same function when the speed reached ten miles per hour, but that was of very little comfort as she looked at the chauffeur's shaven neck and the way his cap was placed precisely centrally on his almost square head. Not normally a woman noted for her imagination, she gave herself a mental shake, but couldn't rid herself of a small worm of dread lurking deep in the pit of her stomach.

The journey seemed endless and she was only able to endure it with to
tolerable equanimity by concentrating on her own breathing and looking out of the window at the sheets of rain. As the day grew darker, the rain grew increasingly sleety and by the time they turned off the autobahn onto what was obviously a private drive it was snowing in earnest. The woman examined her own perfectly manicured fingernails and wondered just what she had allowed herself to be manoeuvred into.

Pushing half a million dollars worth of assistance out of a sticky situation to the back of her mind, she allowed herself to feel misused.

The big car swished to a halt beside a set of ironwork gates. Her driver rolled down his window and said something she didn't catch. The gates slid open and the car picked up speed again. Only now they were driving through a rocky tunnel. She shivered involuntarily. The tunnel was dark and it seemed that the headlights barely pierced the gloom.

"Almost there madam."

That wasn't exactly reassuring either.

Not being a fanciful woman, she wasn't sure why her heart dropped to somewhere in the region of the needle-sharp heels of her boots when the car stopped outside the deeply carved, black walls of an ornate castle. Walls that were being rapidly decorated with white snow frosting. Somewhere in the very back of her mind she heard the words 'Castle of Otranto' and some long-forgotten fear grasped her by the throat. At that moment, had there been anywhere to run she would have fled. But there wasn't. Instead she set her foot on the bottom step and mounted the worn stone steps, bending her mind to grace and suppleness in place of gaucherie and fear.

As she reached the huge doors one leaf was thrown open and a cadaverous figure in the dark suit of a butler stood regarding her. She was a woman well accustomed to servants, so she glided past paying him no more heed than if he had been one of the gargoyles that glowered down on her from the dark stone walls.

Inside the place a huge fire burned in the sort of grate that could have accommodated a whole tree. A servant bustled forward and took her coat. She automatically fluffed her hair and touched fingers to her perfectly painted lips before turning to face the figure that uncurled itself from a huge chair beside that crackling fire. For an instant she saw, or thought she saw, grey scaly skin, yellowish teeth, and long bright claws on strangely articulated fingers. But then the image wavered and all she could really begin to focus on was icy green eyes with vertical slotted pupils. She thought she might have been about to faint, but she was not granted even that small mercy. However, she had never lacked courage and walked to meet her fate with a straight spine and a cool smile.

One week...

One week can be a lifetime or as fleeting as a passing breath.

From that day until the end of a pampered and hugely successful life she could never decide which she experienced. All she knew for certain was that whatever happened to her in those seven days she must have pleased Him greatly to be allowed to leave on her own two feet.

THE PHONE CALL

When the old man shuffled off this mortal coil his only surviving daughter was volunteered (by her tribe of heedless and unruly brothers) to inform the mother whose existence Pa had refused to acknowledge since a particularly acrimonious divorce some thirty years before. Prudence sighed, then picked up the mantle of duty.

Mother had taken the generous financial settlement that made Pa a free agent - a status he took full advantage of - and returned to her own people across the Atlantic in Scotland. And there she had remained —at first in her family's draughty castle, but latterly in a home for bewildered elderlies of aristocratic descent. At least, Prudence thought, she regularly spoke to Mother, so a call shouldn't endanger the old lady's parlous mental state

She shooed her brothers out of the room.

"If I'm doing this I'm doing it without boos and catcalls."

"What does it matter, she's deaf anyway."

"Precisely. Which means I'm going to have enough trouble making her understand without you lot helping."

They went, laughingly playing pushy shovey in the doorway. But at last they were gone and the door was shut behind them.

Prudence dialled, and, after the usual small fuss of arrangement, spoke to the upright old lady whose gradual descent into dementia was more of a sorrow than the death of her blustering ex-husband.

"It's not your usual day to call."

"No. But I have some distressing news."

"You have what?"

"Bad news."

"Bad knees? That's from crawling around after your bastard of a father."

"No Mother. Not knees. News."

The silence was dragging a bit before the old lady spoke again. Her voice sounding thinner and more strained.

"News? Bad news?"

"Yes. I have to tell you that Father died last night."

"Your father lied? But he always lies..."

"Not lied. Died."

"Took a bride? Isn't he a bit old for that kind of foolishness?"

"Not a bride neither. He died."

"What did he cry about."

"He didn't cry. He stopped breathing and died."

"Whyever did he stop breathing? He'll die if he keeps on doing that."

"He did die."

"Why did he do that? What made him think he had fish to fry?"

"Mother. Please try to listen. Last night Father died."

A sharp intake of breath made Ellen think she had got through. But…

"What did he pry into? Your business or the boys?"

"Mother. Can you not understand me? Father is dead."

"Your father has changed his name to Fred?"

"No. He has died. He is deceased. If you weren't a divorcee you'd be a widow."

This time the silence was heavier and more doom laden. While Ellen fought for balance she heard the sound of soft feet on the institutional linoleum and the gentle voice of one of the nurses.

"Your daughter is telling you that her father is dead."

"Oh dear. But he was a monster. Pru can you hear me? I'm sorry I misunderstood and thank you for telling me. Although I can't bring myself to much care."

"No. I don't expect you to care."

"What about you? Do you care?"

"Not much. I don't think anyone cares much."

Mother's chuckle sounded like dry leaves rustling in the wind. "I don't think he understood caring. I can't say I have any sympathy." She sobered. "Do make sure he's cremated, dear. We wouldn't want him coming back to haunt us."

Prudence pushed down the desire to scream, or giggle at the inconsequentiality of her mother's reaction.

"I'll make sure of that," she said evenly.

"Good."

After a little more small talk Prudence judged it time to ring off as Mother was sounding increasingly tired and frail.

As they signed off, Mother gave vent to her dry leaf chuckle once more.

"I just had the most diverting thought."

"What's that?"

"I outlived the old bastard. How he will have hated that. I think I can die happy now, knowing how badly he wanted me to pass first."

THE SUV

Mom. The K-word made flesh. But me and Seraphim coped. Until...

Daddy bought her a new car.

While the adults stood out on the driveway admiring what looked like a maniacal reimagining of a Sherman tank I sat at the bend of the stairs. Worrying.

I didn't see what I could do until Seraphim came and cuddled in beside me.

"It's awful, Raziel," she said, and her blue, blue eyes were bright with tears. "He's given that madwoman a killing machine and it's all operated from a single key fob."

The idea was instantaneous and horribly workable.

"Do you reckon you could get me that key fob?"

She grinned and ran.

By the time our parents had finished congratulating themselves on their perspicacity, I'd done my thing and the fob was back on its hook.

I waited until Mom and Daddy got into their usual after dinner 'discussion', then I sent a single text.

The behemoth on the driveway came crashing through the front wall of the house.

It wasn't my fault that Mom thought she could stop it by standing in the way screaming, was it?

And our stepmom is a lot less of an embarrassment...

THE WAITING ROOM

It is possible to sit expressionless and outwardly composed, even when you are screaming inside. But it's difficult, and most of the occupants of the waiting room fidgeted, or rocked to and fro, or shouted, or made strange animal noises.

The middle-aged woman who sat on the extreme end of one row of seats kept her eyes downcast and her hands folded in her lap.

There were two uniformed female guards behind an armoured mirror screening one corner. The younger elbowed her colleague.

"Why's that one here?"

"Which one?"

"The pale blue cardigan and sensible sandals."

The older woman looked over her spectacles and laughed. "Guess."

"I can't imagine. I mean. She looks as sane as my Auntie Doris."

"She looks as sane as anybody's Auntie Doris, but she's here isn't she."

As if to deliberately prevent further conversion, a fracas broke out in the corner where the toys were stored. The press of a button brought security barrelling in to break up the fight over a pink plush teddy bear. It was noticeable that they gave the woman in the blue cardigan a wide berth as they firmly seated a fat man in shorts as far away as possible from an elderly lady who sported a nappy and a wig of golden curls.

When they left, closing the door firmly behind them, the older guard touched her young companion on the shoulder.

"Before you ask. No. It doesn't get any easier. But it puts food on the table."

Her colleague swallowed and managed a nod.

"How are they all here?" she whispered .

"Money and privilege. If they had come from lesser families they would have been culled at birth, but the rich ones don't produce enough babies for that to happen, so they let them grow up. But if they become 'difficult' they send them here. The doctors always pretend there's hope..."

"Hope for what?"

"I dunno. But, realistically, if we aren't very careful, the only 'hope' is that they will kill each other in one of the quarrels that break out with depressing regularity."

The long morning wore on, and one by one the patients walked, crawled, ran, or were wheeled, into the rooms where the psychologists, physicians, psychics, researchers, and downright quacks awaited them. At the end, only blue cardigan waited. The moment she was alone, she removed a piece of violent purple knitting from the handbag that had been sitting unnoticed by her feet and began industriously clicking away with the needles.

As soon as the knitting came out of the bag the older guard picked up a red telephone and spoke urgently to whoever was at the other end.

"Priscilla's got a handbag, and knitting needles."

The swearing at the other end of the line was sulphurous. "I'm gonna kill that fragging occupational therapist."

"Never mind that right now. She's next."

"Right. Lock the treatment room doors. We're on our way."

The guard thumbed a button and all the lights on the treatment room doors went red. She lifted another phone.

"No need to worry. We have a situation in the waiting room. I'll unlock as soon as security has it under control."

"What? Why?"

"Because she's one of the ones who can never be allowed anything sharp."

The younger woman subsided, watching the wholly absorbed knitter with unhappy eyes. She didn't know what was going to happen next but she was pretty sure she wouldn't like it. Instead of loud shouty barrelling to the rescue, this time the security guys came in quietly - if mob handed. There must have been twenty of them. Two with tranquilliser guns at the ready.

"Pretty knitting Priscilla." The biggest guy spoke in an almost unfeasibly deep voice. "You gonna let me see it?"

Priscilla gave no sign that she had even noticed the men. Although the pace with which she clacked the needles together became even more frantic.

"Come on love. You know you can't keep it."

"Must finish this cardigan for Mama. It's her birthday tomorrow."

"Is that so? You got some pretty paper in your bag to wrap it up with?"

"No. Not allowed paper. Priscilla is a naughty girl. She doesn't get paper. But I have got this."

She reached for the bag and the big guy took advantage of her moment of inattention. He grabbed the knitting and threw it to a colleague before snatching the handbag up from the floor. Priscilla looked up at him and the young guard could see tears welling up in her faded blue eyes.

"Please don't take Priscilla's things."

"Sorry, love. Rules is rules."

Priscilla started to cry in earnest and her thin shoulders heaved with emotion.

The young guard felt that somebody should be comforting this poor, lost soul and it made her angry that so many big men just stood and watched the outpouring of sorrow.

While she was processing her anger and trying to shove it aside - to the place where she was already keeping fear and revulsion - something in the crying woman's posture changed.

Priscilla appeared to be drawing herself in, as if poised to spring into action. Although what one small woman could do against twenty grown men....

Quite a lot as it turned out. One minute she seemed just a pathetic, defeated middle-aged child. The next instant, she became a screaming fighting virago whose hitherto hidden madness was now on full view. It was frightening and if it hadn't been for the bulletproof glass, the young guard might have run. As it was she couldn't stop looking, try though she might. Priscilla leapt for the big man who had taken 'her' knitting. He caught her mid jump, but couldn't keep a hold of the wriggling, kicking, biting figure and she squirmed out of his grasp going after the man who held the disputed knitting, with all the subtlety of an avenging angel or the pet demon of a mad sorcerer. Her clawed hands scraped at his eyes, and it was fortunate for him that her fingers were nail-less because otherwise she would have raked out his eyeballs before anyone was able to subdue her.

They took her down surprisingly gently, even though she must have bitten at least one of them by the spraying blood that coated her face before the men got a proper hold of her. When she was down it took six men to keep her on the floor - two on each leg and one at each wrist - even then she kept on fighting and squirming and shrieking on a high ear-hurting note. The original guy knelt by her head.

"You going to behave now, Priscilla? I don't want to have Jerry there give you a tranq shot."

She stared at him through sightless eyes and it seemed as if she was too far gone to be reached, but he kept on talking to her in his deep, calm voice until she stopped thrashing about and ceased her dreadful mindless screams.

They sat her up and one of the men strapped her elbows together behind her back before taking a leather mask, with eye and nose holes and a barred mouthpiece, out of his pocket. He fitted the device to her head while she stared emptily out of the eye holes.

Once she was restrained, the security guys lifted her to her feet and dusted her down with practised kindliness. They perp-walked the skinny woman towards the exit which entailed them walking past the guards' mirrored enclosure. Priscilla smiled at herself in the mirror and the young guard caught a glimpse of teeth filed to needle points.

"Pretty."

Priscilla preened herself and the security guy's blood shone scarlet against the strong whiteness of her teeth.

"A judge ordered her declawed because she ripped her mother to shreds with her nails. But neither he nor her family will agree to having her teeth removed."

The young guard lost her lunch in a convenient litter bin.

Drake was determined to stand his ground.

"We gotta keep watch twenty-four seven," he insisted

The ship's captain, fresh out of the Academy, still water-plump and pink-cheeked, and spit and polish to his eyebrows, stared at the skinny unprepossessing figure of the ship's engineer. He winced at the oil under the older man's fingernails, and his stooped, crablike walk.

"And if I say that is unnecessary?"

"Then you'm as stupid as you'm green."

Lieutenant Heronimus Wilkins stuck out his beardless chin, but before he could make a fatal mistake a frightened scream drew his attention to the view screen at the front end of the brand-new Swordfish-class cruiser they were space testing. He couldn't miss the magnitude of the lump of twisted and pockmarked metal that was floating inexorably towards his command. But how would he react? Wilkins made one of the better decisions of his short life.

"What should we do, engineer?"

Drake took the con and eased the nimble cruiser out of harm's way. He stood up.

"Now. Where was we?"

"You were giving me some excellent advice, which I was about to be stupid enough to ignore. I think I just learned the error of my ways."

"Thank frag for that."

Wilkins' smile was complicated, but he was trying.

"How did that thing get so close?"

Drake sighed "It got close because some bliddy fool turned off the early warning system."

The biggest and most arrogant of the ensigns lifted a careless shoulder.

"It was getting on my tits," he said and sloped off.

Drake bent to examine the EWS, it was worse than he had hoped. "That bliddy wossname never turned the system off. He broke it."

Wilkins crouched at his side, where even a complete greenhorn could see the damage.

"Can you repair it?"

"Maybe. Or maybe I can jury rig something."

A lot of hard work later the bleeping had returned, offering some measure of protection from space junk at least.

Wilkins brought Drake a cup of hot broth and crouched beside the exhausted engineer who was feeling the effects of six hours on his knees in a restricted crawl space whose outside wall was so cold he'd had to operate with rags tied around his knees and elbows for fear of frostbite.

"Thank gods you're familiar with deep space, engineer."

Drake sighed. "I been out here more times than I can comfortably count, but as to bein' 'familiar'? No. It don't pay to feel as if you'm familiar with deep space. If you do the bitch'll get you."

Wilkins nodded. "I felt that when the wrecksteroid was bearing down on us. It feels pitiless out here."

"Pitiless is about right." Drake scratched his head. "What I don't understand, though, is how come you lot is out here, test flying a brand-new cruiser, without a seasoned flier among you."

"Me neither," Wilkins said miserably. "Me neither."

Drake tried to be reassuring. "Maybe between us we can bring baby home safe."

"That's a big maybe. But we can try. You go and get some rest. I'll leave the ship on autopilot and take the watch."

Drake nodded and all but crawled to his cot. He was asleep almost before his head hit the pillow. It wasn't long enough later, though, when the EWS stopped bleeping cheerily and started screaming. Drake flung his skinny legs out of his cot and ran into the cockpit. Tuning a camera to the protesting sensor brought up a picture on the screen in front of the vacant pilot's seat.

"Fraggit," he said flatly, "that's about all we bloody need."

He was buck naked, and unimpressive at the best of times, but the multicoloured monstrosity on screen seemed to leech away any shred of vitality as he looked.

"What is it?"

"It's one of them circuses what does the rounds of the asteroid belt, playing the mines and prisons and the like."

Wilkins stared at the image. "Yes. I can see crude pictures of circus acts and animals, and stuff. And there's pictures of women"

Drake coloured miserably. Wilkins took pity on him.

"Okay. But.What do we do about it?"

"I'd like to pretend we never saw it. But we can't do it because the message will already have been sent."

"What message?"

"Automatic notification. That there is a vessel where there shouldn't oughter be one. So we gotta check it out"

"I didn't know about that."

"No. I don't reckon you did. Seems to me nobody told you nothing."

"They didn't. So I'm very glad you are here. Tell me, what do we do about that thing?"

"You puts on your prettiest uniform and makes what they calls a courtesy call. You asks nicely if'n you can see their papers. Which they won't have. You looks stern. They promises to get papers at their next stop. Then, with only average luck, you comes back here and we waves them on their way."

"Sounds like a plan to me. But would we be as accommodating if we had a full crew and the weapons bay was operational?"

"Yup. Them bastards over there has Galactic Militia over a barrel and they knows it."

"How's that?"

"You ever been on an asteroid?"

Wilkins shook his head.

"Me neither. But I knows a few what has. Them circus ships brings entertainment, and women, which is all that keeps a lid on thousands of hard men trapped in deep space. If the ships stopped coming the asteroid belt'd go up in flames."

Wilkins pinched the bridge of his nose. "Okay. If I go over there, will you stay here?"

"Yup. You couldn't pay me to visit."

"I'm not going to ask why. And I'm glad you'll stay with the ship."

An hour later, the detail was ready to visit the huge 'circus' ship. Captain Wilkins and four of the steadier graduates boarded a nifty little flitter and crossed the blackness to where a port was open and waiting for them.

Wilkins returned some while later. His uniform was as stiffly pressed as ever, but his round, pink face bore a look of deep disquiet. He joined Drake in the cockpit and shut the door.

"I have just had the most peculiar time of my life. As soon as I set foot on that ship, I felt as if something alien was inside my head."

"Hear tell that's to do with mirrors and music, and smells."

"Maybe. I could smell women. It was distracting. But it's more than that. I couldn't properly see the circus people, it was as if my eyes didn't want to focus properly."

He went over to the captain's chair and stood deep in thought .

Drake kept silent, letting the young officer settle.

Wilkins sighed. "I'm pretty sure we only left because we were permitted to, and that frightens me. The setup of that thing pulls at you like forbidden fruit. I think the person they call ringmaster found me amusing enough that they invited me for supper later."

"And what did you say?"

"Apologised profusely, saying we had a ship to space test and a very tight schedule."

"You reckon you got away with it?"

"I don't know, but maybe. They were polite enough not to press the issue. Were more interested in Swordfish's armament if I don't miss my guess. I'm not proud of myself, but I lied. Pretended the armoury was stocked. And the gun port covers hid more than fresh air."

"Well done lad. Shall we get out of here?"

"Please."

Drake set autopilot for the coordinates from where they could turn and head back to spaceport and pulled the throttles halfway. Wilkins looked at his tired face and offered a smile.

"Go back to bed, engineer."

Drake went gratefully.

He was awoken by the instincts years on spaceships had honed to a keen edge screaming 'danger'. At first his sleep-befuddled brain couldn't grab a handle on what was wrong, but when it did, realisation came as a hammer blow. It was dark on a ship where darkness was the enemy, and silent as a graveyard on Walpurgis Night. If he wasn't wrong, and he was rarely wrong about such matters, Swordfish's engines had ceased to function, as had the generator that provided light, heat, and fresh air. To all intents and purposes the cruiser was a lump of dead metal, drifting in the killing vacuum of deep space

He lifted his head and listened, and just as the menacing quality of the silence had scraped his every nerve ending raw, the sound of heavy booted feet on metal told him he wasn't alone. The boots ran, stumbling, past his cubby and the sound of rasping breaths was loud in the thickening dark. With the boots gone, he could just about catch another, smaller, sound if he listened hard. It was a sort of scratchy scraping, almost as if clawed rodent feet prowled the gangways in search of prey. Rodent feet? On a space ship? He slapped his forehead with a calloused palm and ordered himself to get a grip before sitting up fully and feeling for trousers and boots. Once dressed he groped for, and found, his tool belt, which he fitted around his skinny hips. Not that he had any real expectation of tools being helpful, he just felt less vulnerable with the belt on.

As he stood up, the quiet was torn apart by a scream compounded of agony and fear.

"Help, help!"

It was a female voice, and he remembered that a couple of the ensigns were young girls. Some ingrained pattern of chivalry had him running towards the sound. He followed the sound of heartbroken sobs and just as he rounded a bend in the walkway someone managed to engage the auxiliary generator and the greenish emergency lighting blinked slowly into action. The girl screamed again, and he poured on as much speed as his legs could afford.

She was scrunched as far into a ball as it's possible for a human to get, bleeding heavily from one small, bare foot. Drake heard scrabbling again, and as his head snapped around he thought he caught sight of something grey and rodentine with a long pink tail disappearing into an air duct.

But there was no time to waste on hallucinations, he needed to help the wounded girl. There was a first aid kit on the wall twenty paces to his right and he wrenched it open, grabbing a field dressing and a pressure syringe. He wrapped her foot and sealed the dressing tight, but not before he realised she was missing two toes and it almost looked as if they had been bitten off.

He dredged up a smile. "There that'll stop the bleeding. You need a pain injection?"

She sat upright and rubbed a shaking hand over her close cropped hair. "No. Thank you. I hate those things. They make me all fuzzy. And I've already had a motherfucker of a nightmare. Now I'm awake I'd like to stay that way."

Drake thought she'd probably been awake all along, but judged it best not to voice that thought.

"Okay, I'll just give you an antibiotic shot."

The girl winced as the drug was injected into her thigh, but bore the burn bravely. He helped her to her feet.

"Hang on to me and we'll find out where the rest are."

Drake and his companion moved carefully, and she was doing fine until the sound of scrabbling ran overhead. She cringed and hid her face against his shoulder.

"It's the rats," she whispered.

Drake gave her the only comfort he could offer. "There are no rats in space." Which made little sense given the nature of her injury, but she lifted her face and plastered on a smile.

They moved away from the crew cabins, but it wasn't until they neared the cockpit that the sound of boots on metal let them know they weren't alone.

Wilkins voice called from up ahead. "Is that you engineer?"

"It is. Me and…"

"Ensign Beta #6."

"Oh, good. That's almost all of us, then."

"Almost?"

"Yeah, we're missing Ensign Theta #1. The idiot who broke the EWS."

They rounded the corner to see Wilkins with a blaster in either hand.

Beta #6 saluted.

"Somebody ran past me screaming. Pushed me over so the rats could get me."

"Sounds like his level of brave. But? Rats?"

The sound of scrabbling claws overhead brought him up short.

Drake looked upward.

"There's something up there, right enough, but I ain't sure what."

In the cockpit, the ensigns clung together like the babies they were, all looking to Drake for the comfort he couldn't give.

"Somebody give me a lift into that duct up there and I'll see if I can jury rig some kind of drive to get us home."

The tallest lad made a back and Drake scrambled into the ship's wiring harness, or what was left of it. Every wire had been stripped of its insulation then bitten through. It was hopeless, but how does a man tell a dozen kids they are about to die. While he was chewing on that bit of gristle, Swordfish started to move with purpose. He felt a flare of hope, but beat it back as ridiculous. As abruptly as she had started to move the ship stopped. Came the sound of screaming metal, the hiss of an airlock, and the squawk of hurdy-gurdy music. The next thing he heard was a blaster being discharged at full power, then another.

"Your devices do not work on my people," the voice was coolly amused.

Someone must have tried to rush the speaker, as there was a sort of a sizzling noise followed by the sound of something heavy hitting the ground.

Drake risked crawling to where a burnt-out light fitting offered a porthole of charred plexiglas. The crew was lined up against the wall and a group of amorphous creatures, whose constantly shifting shapes extruded limbs and features at need, was chaining them together with effortless efficiency. The lump on the floor that was surely Wilkins groaned, and one of the creatures dragged him to the end of the line, chaining him securely.

One figure stood alone not far from Drake's vantage point it seemed to have no difficulty holding its form though Drake was glad he could only see its back. It whistled a high note that hurt his ears, and seven grey rats appeared as if from nowhere.

"Is this all of them, my pets?"

They twittered, and two of the subordinate creatures marched off, returning quickly with Theta #1 held firmly in their pincers.

They stepped back and the tall ensign bowed so low his nose all but touched his knees. "Greetings Great One. I have codes for all areas and plans of the ship's systems. All can be yours."

"And what would you in return."

"My life and freedom."

"What of your friends?"

"They are no friends of mine. Merely subordinate creatures whose fate interests me not."

The creature made a noise in the back of its throat. "This one is contemptible, even for a meat animal . Dispose of it and we shall feast soon."

#1 screamed. Just once before a blob picked him up by his heels and held him high enough so he hung like a side of cow meat in a rich planet market. Another alien being silenced his screaming with a diagonal slash across the throat. His blood sprayed the cockpit with a fine mist of red, and the girl Drake had rescued crumpled in a faint.

The rats chittered some more and their master bent to touch each grey head. "Fret not about the old one, my pretties, its flesh will be too tough for our enjoyment and it is not prime enough for the breeding program. Leave it here. Let it die in its own time without heat or the air its kind needs to breathe. Take the rest and we shall discover their fate in due time."

The chained figures were dragged away without unnecessary cruelty but with equally without any mercy.

The master alien was the last to leave, pulling around it the simulation of humanity it stared up at the light fitting where Drake lay.

When it had gone and the airlock had closed behind it, Swordfish was ejected from the circus ship to tumble end over end in the ruthless cold.

When Drake managed to disentangle his bruised and battered body from the wrecked technology and made it to what had been the floor of the cockpit, the air was already getting depleted. It hurt his chest to breathe, and his mind had started to play the cruel tricks of oxygen deprivation.

Standing alone among the blood and debris he was sure that the red eyes of the rats watched him from the corners of the room. As he felt their sharp claws climb his body towards his unprotected throat he threw back his head and screamed until his throat was raw.

With little time left to make any decisions, he thought to leave a message for anyone who might some day find the wreck. Dipping his finger in the puddle of congealing blood, where a human had been butchered like a goat, he wrote carefully on the wall.

It took a long time, but when he finished he laughed at his own wit before putting a blaster to his head and ending the agony forever.

The reddish brown letters stalked the walls like alien creatures as the man who wrote them died.

'There are no Rats in Space.'

HOPE

The spirits of the woodland felt the pain of their holy places dwindling under the assault of the human machines, but they were patient beings who bided their time and watched. They saw the rise of the arrogant ones with their fat bellies and careless cruelty, and they also foresaw the fall from grace engendered by such greed and stupidity.

Knowing that the end game was afoot and with the feeling in their souls that their children had a part to play in the plans of Mother Earth, they sent one of their own precious young ones to the place where the wealthiest of the humans raised their own younglings. Flora cast down her eyes and did as the spirits commanded, even knowing her own chance of motherhood was taken from her by the needs of of the forest beneath her feet.

She was 'welcomed' at the place and given the dirtiest and most menial of tasks to do. Working only for her bed and board she became the most trusted of all those whose destiny was to care for the young whose parents found those tasks beneath their greatness. She was a quiet creature, but one who listened and understood more than the untroubled brown eyes ever showed. She heard the pontifications of the 'doctors' and the priests as the fertility of the human race fell away. She kept her face calm when the silverbacks in their expensive suits declared this to be a punishment of god on women who no longer knew their place. She smiled inwardly when the scientists explained that this could not be the case, citing the deformity of the male seed as the primary cause. But she could not hold back the tears of pity when the soldiers came and took the foremost scientist of all from his office in the nursery. They burned that venerable old man alive, and his screams sounded to Flora like the first death cries of the human race.

Some days, when she looked at the innocent younglings in her care and she saw how sickly they were becoming, she cursed those who sent her to witness the end. Of course, she didn't live long enough to see the game through (even forest folk do not live that long), and when she became too old to work her place was taken by a sturdy youngster with broad shoulders and a plain face. The humans named this person Bessie - thinking Salicis Arbore far too fanciful a name for a servant.

Bessie wasn't as amenable as Flora and the humans feared her a little so that when she announced that she was taking Flora home to die nobody argued. Only the oldest among the matrons even daring to ask if she would return.

"I will. If you will get out of my way now."

The human woman moved aside.

Bessie carried the dying Flora into the forest, walking for many days until she found the grove of trees that remembered Flora as a sapling. She laid her frail burden down on the rich loam. As Flora faded away her memories flooded Bessie's mind and and her voice spoke in the silence.

"The last of them must be saved."

Then she was gone.

Bessie trudged back to the nursery, stubbornly set on the route of duty but with a heaviness in her heart.

Fifty years of hard labour passed, while the world around the place of the younglings changed almost beyond recognition. The forest retreated and the cruel sun now beat down on an ochre-coloured desert, wherein the grey building occupied the only oasis for a thousand miles. And still the human race plundered and pillaged. And still they had no luck reversing their infertility.

So matters stood when Bessie - now the only adult left in the place, whose sole job was to look after the only human cub born in a decade - received a pilotless drone with a package containing her instructions. She felt the heaviness that her heart had known since the day of Flora's death rise up and almost choke her. The silverbacks had decided the fate of the youngling they had named Hope. And it wasn't to be kind.

She waited until moonrise before walking quietly out into the garden. Accessing the memories Flora passed to her she could see the days when there had been maybe a hundred human cubs playing in the kindly moonlight. But now there was just the one lonely youngster swinging on the rope swing over the lake. The one that there used to be such a big queue for. The shadow of simple happiness as it swung across the water made Bessie's heart hurt for she had come to love this human as much as if it had been her own seedling planted in the forest loam.

Sensing her approach Hope turned and called joyously.

"See how high I can swing. I think I can almost touch the sky."

"Indeed you can, loved one. Indeed you can."

She tried to keep her voice light and cheerful but there was no fooling Hope. The youngling stopped swinging and came to sit in the grass at her side.

"Tell me, Bessie. What is it that you know? What makes you so sad on this beautiful night?"

Perhaps she should have lied or dissembled, but she had not the heart or the skill to fool the clear-sighted intelligence that lived in the head that seemed almost too big for Hope's slender neck.

"Because you appear genderless, they have decided they can make you a female. I have been given the hormones to put in your foodstuffs. And when you grow breasts they will take you to try and impregnate you with their poisoned seed." A tear fell, and Hope put a gentle had on the shoulder of its kindly nursemaid.

"Does this mean that now is the time?"

"It does. If you have the courage."

"It's not a case of courage. It's more a case of being realistic. If I am the last of my race so be it. If I am not prepared to be made the subject of their experimentation..."

"Truly spoken. Tomorrow then. In the heat of the sun..."

Hope leaned on the shoulder of the only being that had ever offered unconditional friendship and sighed.

"How did we come to this?"

Bessie thought for a while. "I don't rightly know. What I do know is that the greed and savagery of some of your race brought them to a place of power, which they have continually abused, handing their entitlement down from generation to generation. Only now they have nobody to pass it to. Which is why you are so important. You must understand that you are not just the only human youngling around here, you are the only human youngling anywhere on the breast of the earth."

"Are you sure, Bessie?"

"More or less. The other two I knew of haven't survived whatever was done to them."

"Oh. I see." Hope turned a pair of weary eyes to Bessie's palely moonlit face. "If I'm so important, why did everyone but you run away?"

"Fear mostly. At first they thought you wouldn't survive. So a lot ran away for fear of the punishment if you died. Then you weren't the female child the preachers prophesied. So another slew headed for the hills. And so on."

"Why did you stay? My own kind abandoned me. But you stayed. Why?"

"At first I remained for the sake of duty. But soon it became love. And there is no greater force than love."

"So will you come with me tomorrow then?"

"Of course I will. You'd not survive the desert without me and my hunting skills." She took the smooth roundness of Hope's face in her two rough palms. "We will do it together. But for now how about using your catapult on the three camera drones that are buzzing about the place."

The next morning as the sun turned the desert every shade of rosy pink and silver, two figures left the shelter of the nursery. They wore cloaks the colour of the desert sand and carried stout walking poles. A week later they stood atop a spiny ridge and Bessie laid a hand on Hope's arm.

"Take a last look, loved one. From now on you will be unable to see the place of your birth."

Hope looked back soberly.

"I wonder if there will ever be children there again."

Bessie shrugged and they moved away, disturbing nothing as they made their careful way.

By any reckoning they had been around half a year walking when the landscape began to change. Hope breathed deeply.

"What is that smell."

"It's the earth. The smell of fertile lands. I honestly never thought we'd get here. See the ribbon of silver in the distance. That's the great river and beyond it is the forest where we will be safe." Then Bessie looked at her companion fully. "Not that anyone would recognise you now."

Indeed it was hard to reconcile the thin child on the rope swing with the brown hard youngling whose body moved with oiled ease, at one with the earth and at ease with self.

Hope laughed, low and amused. "No. I have changed somewhat. Not least by becoming a full male. I don't understand how that happened."

"It'll be the water. The place where you were had much female hormone in the water from all the women who had lived there." A strange voice spoke from quite close and Bessie felt for her knife. "No knife needed my sister. I am a watcher from the old gods - those who sent first Flora then she who is named for a willow tree to guide and guard the last human."

"Show yourself then." Hope spoke harshly.

"It cannot. If it is truly what it says its body is far away under a tree somewhere and only it's awareness is here. There is only one way to tell."

Bessie nicked her own thumb with her sharp blade and let three drops of blood fall to the earth. Something screamed and they were vouchsafed sight of a half-naked youngling tied to a tree.

"He speaks sooth." Bessie rubbed her thumb with a piece of aloe vera from her pack. "I expect we will see a welcoming party in a few days."

"Why was he tied to that tree?"

"To anchor his spirit while his awareness roamed."

"Oh. I see."

And Bessie rather thought he did see.

While the rest of humanity dragged out its days among the drugs and the plastics and the desperation, Hope grew to manhood in the forest where he learned to respect and understand the earth on which his two feet stood. In the fullness of time he took a mate from among the forest females and the young of the young of his young played around his legs before he was taken to his rest.

The earth healed and the forest took back her own.

One night a band of travellers stepped out of the woods into a clearing where a pile of grey stone gave evidence of where a building once stood. One of the younglings found a rope swing still attached to the boughs of a venerable tree.

"Look Mama," he shouted, "look how high I can swing."

As his mother looked, his shadow on the water awoke some dormant racial memory and she turned to her mate.

"I think this is a holy place. It seems to me to be where hope was born."

If you enjoyed this book please consider leaving a review or visiting author.to/janejago for more stories and poetry

Printed in Great Britain
by Amazon

34352374R00040